The Duke of Hearts

(THE 1797 CLUB BOOK 7)

By

*USA Today Bestseller
Jess Michaels*

THE DUKE OF HEARTS
The 1797 Club Book 7
www.1797Club.com

Copyright © Jesse Petersen, 2018

ISBN-13: 978-1987759488
ISBN-10: 1987759486

For more information, contact Jess Michaels
www.AuthorJessMichaels.com

To contact the author:
Email: Jess@AuthorJessMichaels.com
Twitter www.twitter.com/JessMichaelsbks
Facebook: www.facebook.com/JessMichaelsBks

Jess Michaels raffles a gift certificate EVERY month to members of her newsletter, so sign up on her website:
http://www.authorjessmichaels.com/

DEDICATION

For Leora Hansen. A true embodiment of class, dedication and kindness. Thank you for all you did for the hundreds of students who loved you. Rest well, dear friend.

And for Michael, who I met in her class. Debate kids make the best marriages.

CHAPTER ONE

Spring 1812

It could have been called a 1797 Club party, thanks to the number of friends Matthew Cornwallis, Duke of Tyndale, had in attendance. Dukes abounded, in seemingly every corner. Once upon a time, he would have enjoyed this moment when they were all together. It had become so rare over the years as his friends grew into their titles, their marriages, their responsibilities. But at present, it was not joy in Matthew's heart as he watched them from a distance.

It was something far darker, far uglier. Something he did not wish to name. More than half of his friends were here with their wives. They spun around the dancefloor in pairs, eyes locked, hands inappropriately low, laughter echoing, cheeks filling with color thanks to whispered words.

They were all happy. He should have been happy for them. He was. And he wasn't. Because he was standing on the outside now, looking in on a world he should have joined years ago. Except Angelica had died.

All he was left with were regrets.

Suddenly Robert Smithton, Duke of Roseford, slid up beside him. Wordlessly he handed Matthew a scotch and then lifted his own glass to clink it against Matthew's.

"To the bachelors," he said, staring out at the dancefloor and their friends. "Those of us left, that is."

Matthew shut his eyes. There were days when his grief still felt so raw, no matter how many years had passed since the death of his fiancée. Today was one of them, and Robert's words were like a knife in his heart.

"Sorry," Robert said softly.

Matthew's eyes flew open and he stared at his friend. Robert was almost his polar opposite, a man driven by pleasure and nothing more. He didn't allow deeper emotions, so he never experienced the pain that went with them.

But he was also a brilliant mind, a loyal friend and someone Matthew cared deeply for, regardless of his judgment of Robert's decisions.

"I must look like hell if *you're* apologizing to me," Matthew croaked out before he took a sip of his drink.

The tension on Robert's face bled away and he grinned, the rogue in full force at that moment. "I'm apologizing because I'm an ass," he said. "But you know that. You're always telling me much the same."

Matthew drew in a deep breath as the pain faded a fraction. Leave it to Robert to do that. He did appreciate it.

"Well, you're no more an ass than usual," he said softly. "So I forgive you this once."

Robert tipped his head. "Much obliged, Your Grace."

Matthew sighed as his attention returned to the others. The music had faded now and they were joining up in little clusters, the women comparing gowns and smiling at their husbands. Every once in a while, Ewan, Duke of Donburrow, brushed his hand over his wife Charlotte's swollen pregnant belly, and a shadow of a smile crossed his normally serious face.

"It's the end of an era," Robert mused.

Matthew jolted from his own thoughts and nodded. "I suppose it is. They have all found their matches, leaving only a handful of us without such happiness. But it was bound to happen, wasn't it? We're of an age to do such things. Someone will be next."

Robert snorted out a laugh of derision. "It won't bloody

well be me," he said, and downed his entire drink in one slug. Matthew laughed with him. "No, my assumption is that you will be last—you enjoy your life too much to surrender it willingly."

For a brief moment, a shadow crossed Robert's face. Matthew tilted his head at the sight of it, for it was an expression he'd never seen before on his old friend. Before he could press, Hugh Margolis, Duke of Brighthollow and another of their bachelor friends, approached.

Matthew's concern shifted. In the past six months, he'd seen a change in Hugh. His hair had grown out, his cheeks were slashed with stubble more often than not. More than that, there was something deeply troubled in his dark gaze. Whenever he was asked about it, he waved the question off.

But tonight some of that trouble seemed faded. He grinned at his friends, back to the light and lively companion he'd always been. He even slung an arm around Robert. "And what are you two talking about so seriously, eh?"

Robert rolled his eyes. "How very romantic our friends have all become. We were debating who would enter the snare of marriage next." He winked at Matthew. "*And* we were discussing how miserable Tyndale is."

Hugh's smile fell and his expression gentled. "Are you very miserable, Tyndale?"

Matthew shook his head. It was a funny thing. Once you lost someone, it was like you turned to glass. Everyone else tiptoed around, trying not to upset or break anything. He was growing tired of it, in truth.

"It's been three years," he said softly. "I suppose Robert is right that I ought to be over the loss by now and not roaming around like the maudlin hero of a romantic novel."

Robert shrugged. "In my experience, ladies trip over themselves for a maudlin hero. You must start using it to your advantage."

Matthew couldn't picture doing anything of the kind, but he played along for Robert's sake. "And how do you suggest I do that?"

It was like he'd offered his friend a thousand pounds, Roseford's eyes lit up so bright. He was practically bouncing as he said, "Let's get out of this stuffy party and go somewhere fun."

Hugh shook his head. "I shudder to think what you define as fun, my friend. Where exactly do you mean?"

Robert grinned wider. "The Donville Masquerade."

Matthew stared at him, his mouth slightly agape. "The sex club," he said with a shake of his head. God's teeth, everyone knew about the Donville Masquerade.

Robert drew back. "You limit yourself, my dear old friend. Not just a sex club. There's drink, gaming and dancing, and yes, I think a night with a comely lady would do each of us good."

"Christ," Hugh said with a slight laugh. "You and your appetites."

Robert wrinkled his brow. "And since when is indulging in pleasure such a terrible appetite? It can't have been so long since you did the same."

Hugh shifted. "Well...nine months," he admitted.

Robert's eyes went impossibly wide and his mouth twisted in horror. "No. That...can't be true. Is that even possible? Matthew, tell him that he will turn into a monk if he doesn't change his ways."

The two men faced Matthew and now it was his cheeks that filled with color. "I doubt I'm the one to tell him such, considering how long it's been for me."

Robert drew back. "Longer than nine months?"

Matthew cleared his throat. "I'm not sure this is a proper topic—"

"Ten months?" Robert pressed. "A year?"

"Honestly, Roseford, you are—"

"More than a year?" Robert nearly recoiled into the crowd.

Matthew let out a long sigh. He knew his bulldog of a friend, and there was no way he'd let this go until he had uncovered the number. "Fine. Three and a half years."

Robert gaped, unspeaking. Even Hugh jerked his face toward Matthew like he'd declared he had decided to take over Spain. Matthew pursed his lips and forced himself to remain impassive beneath their horrified expressions.

"How are you both not...*dead?*" Robert said. "You *are* dead, for that sounds like living in a grave."

"Roseford," Hugh said, voice heavy with warning.

Robert waved him off. "It's settled, we're going to the Donville Masquerade tonight. I have a membership and you two will come as my guests. I shall brook no refusals."

With that, he turned on his heel and strode from the ballroom, likely to call for his carriage.

Matthew stared at Hugh and found him looking back. Brighthollow shrugged. "He isn't entirely wrong, you know."

"Of course he isn't," Matthew said. "He never is. Not entirely."

"We probably both could use a break from our troubles. Nothing says you have to spend an evening with a lightskirt, after all."

Matthew shifted. He rarely thought about sinful things anymore. Those thoughts had seemed so wrong after Angelica's death. Eventually he'd just purged them from his mind and become the monk Robert had first accused Hugh of being.

"You're right," he said with a sigh. "And I'll go, if only to keep him from having an apoplexy in the middle of James and Emma's ballroom."

They moved to say their goodbyes to their friends, but Hugh caught his arm before they could reach anyone. He tugged Matthew to face him and his expression was serious.

"You aren't betraying her," he said softly.

Matthew's lips parted and he nodded. "I know."

Except that wasn't true. What Robert wanted from him felt exactly like a betrayal of the woman he had once loved, the one he'd lost. And that's why he had no intention of doing it. Not even when surrounded by "temptation" at the wicked Donville Masquerade.

Isabel Hayes straightened her mask before the door to the hack opened and a bored servant offered her a hand down. He took a few coins from her for the driver and motioned her toward the entrance of a dull looking building with an elaborately carved door.

Only Isabel knew that there was nothing boring about this place. And nothing ordinary.

She stepped into the foyer and found the regular man standing at a high table, a book balanced on its surface. "Good evening, miss. Your name or arranged name?"

Isabel shifted. She certainly wasn't going to use her real name here of all places. "Miss Swan," she said, and her cheeks felt hot with the lie.

He scanned over the book and made a little mark. "Good evening, Miss Swan. Welcome to the Donville Masquerade."

As he said those words, he came around to a secondary door and swung it open wide, allowing her in to the inner sanctum of the place.

Immediately, she tensed. That was always her reaction when she entered this home of sin and seduction and wicked pleasures that women such as herself were not supposed to crave.

And yet she did. Desperately.

The first room was a wide, open gambling hall, and she stepped inside. She'd been here three times, if she counted tonight. And she was still nervous as her eyes scanned the hall.

Some of it was what one might expect. There were tables scattered about and men and women playing games at them. Normal, if scandalous. But there was more, too. Against one wall, a lady and a gentleman leaned together, kissing wildly as his hands ran over her body. On one of the tables, a couple was copulating like animals right out in the open as a handful of men watched and cheered.

Isabel's stomach fluttered at the sight, her own body aching as she edged around the room, trying to stay small so she wouldn't be noticed as she watched.

She liked to watch. She'd discovered that scandalous secret about herself some time ago, and this was one place to feed that desire. The *only* place, considering how time was running out for her.

She shook her head, pushing away those unwanted thoughts, and instead leaned against the wall to watch the patrons around her. Watched them talk and kiss, watched anonymous hands go under skirts and cocks be pulled from trousers, watched as some of the couples disappeared down the hallway to slake their needs in the private rooms they paid extra to access, while others didn't wait and had their fill out in the open.

Her knees were already weak and her sex throbbed, but in that moment the atmosphere in the chamber changed. There was a murmur that seemed to touch every part of the crowd and people began to crane their necks toward the entrance. She did the same and saw three masked men had entered the room.

"Excuse me," she said, motioning to one of the servants.

"Yes, miss?" he said, and it didn't escape her notice that his gaze moved up and down her frame. She blushed, for it was one thing to look and another to be seen.

"Wh-who are the men who just entered?"

He looked and shook his head. "I know the one in the middle is the Duke of Roseford. He makes no effort to hide his identity, even though he wears a mask. The others? I don't know, miss. Excuse me."

He moved back off to the crowd and Isabel worried her lower lip as the men entered the chamber. They were all three tall. One had brown hair that was a bit too long and thick with wild curls. The one in the middle, identified as a duke, had an air of confidence and a wicked quirk to his mouth.

But it was the third who caught her eye. He had hair as dark as pitch, close cut. She could not see his eyes thanks to the distance and the mask that shaded them, but he had a well-defined jaw with a hint of a beard, and fine lips.

She jolted. Fine lips? Who in the world called a man's lips *fine*?

She watched as women from the crowd swarmed up to the new arrivals. Most seemed enamored of the duke in the middle, leaning over to him, putting themselves on display as he grinned.

She noted that her mystery man seemed the least interested of the three. Oh, he looked, but he stepped away, as if he wanted to avoid the trouble about to be started by hungry hands and experienced mouths.

She had a less experienced mouth, of course, but she wondered what that man would taste like.

Pivoting, she lifted a hand to her suddenly trembling lips. Great God, what was wrong with her? She came here to watch, not participate. She hadn't the courage to do so, nor the ability to forget all she had been taught as a lady. Well, something like a lady, at any rate.

She certainly wasn't here to wax poetic about a stranger, or determine his taste. That would be unseemly. *He* was here for the lightskirts.

He moved away from his friends into the crowd and she forced herself to put her attention back to what she'd come for. The night was drawing later, and as always, that meant the activities in the room were growing more heated. Gaming became desperate, more and more of the people gave up on it entirely to surrender to their hedonistic needs. She heard the music from the back of the room, where there was a stage for acts so scandalous that they made her knees weak.

And yet, as she watched the games, her mind kept returning to that man at the door. When she watched a man strip a woman's dress open at the front and bury his face in her breasts, she pictured herself in that position, only with a masked man with full lips.

"Hello, pretty lady."

She froze at the sound of a drunken voice beside her. Normally, she was very aware of the other patrons and moved herself out of the way of anyone who leered. But she'd been distracted and now when she turned there was a very large, very drunk, very focused man standing over her, licking his lips as he looked at her.

"What a pretty little chick you are," he drawled. "Looking for a fox to come into your henhouse?"

She stepped back, but the crowd had swelled and there was very little space to be put between then. She forced a smile. "You mistake me, sir, I am not here for…foxes."

He laughed. "Well, if you like hens, I'd pay you ten pounds to watch."

Her eyes widened. That was one thing she hadn't seen during her time here. "N-no," she insisted. "I'm sure there are other ladies who would be pleased at the offer, though. Good night."

She pivoted to walk away and he caught her arm, dragging her back toward him. His eyes were no longer filled with humor, but dark and angry. "You're right, plenty of other ladies would give what I wanted. I chose you, you tart. Now give me what I want."

She pulled against his grip, but he was far too big and strong to escape. "Stop," she said firmly and clearly. "I said no."

"You don't get to say no," he growled.

"I believe she just did."

Isabel gaped in shock, for the very handsome man she had been focused on earlier was the one speaking as he pushed through the crowd. It was as if she'd conjured him. Up close she could see his eyes were a beautiful gray, and right now they were stormy seas, filled with anger at the man holding her.

"You meant it, did you not?" he asked softly, those eyes darting over to her. "You weren't playing a game?"

"No—no," she gasped, even more captivated by the dark, deep resonance of his voice. "I was not playing a game."

The stranger reached out and caught the cad's arm, breaking

9

his grip on her wrist and pulling him away from her. She lifted it, rubbing gently as the stranger put himself between them.

"I cannot imagine you were not read the same rules as we were when you came in here, sir," the stranger said. "The ladies are to be unmolested. To behave as you are is to court banishment, I believe."

Her attacker's eyes narrowed farther. "You work for Rivers, then?" he spat.

"I don't, but I can certainly call someone who does."

"For a whore," the man spat. "A woman who lowers herself to come here and then denies what she's exhibiting for all to see. Whore!"

He shouted the last over the stranger's shoulder toward Isabel, and she turned away in embarrassment.

Now the stranger's posture grew even angrier. He actually seemed bigger as he tugged her attacker close and growled. "This woman has just as much as right as you do to come and go as she pleases. By coming here she did not ask to be molested by a drunken fool. Her desires are no dirtier than your own. Now get out or I will find your way out for you."

He pushed the other man then, sending him staggering into the crowd. Her attacker glared at them, then skulked away.

Now the stranger turned to her, all the anger gone from his expression, replaced with concern. "Are you well? Did he hurt your wrist?"

She glanced down and found that she was still gripping it in her opposite hand. "Oh, n-no," she stammered, working hard to find words, harder than it should have been. "I'm fine. Thank you so much, sir. I cannot think of what I could do to tell you how much I appreciate your interference and your harsh set-down of that lout."

His eyes went a little wider and she blushed slightly as she realized the double entendre of her words. Now she had no idea what he would think of her, and if she had just jumped out of a cozy frying pan and directly into a burning fire.

CHAPTER TWO

Matthew was having a hard time focusing as he stared down into the lovely face of his masked companion. Her delicate features were impossible to hide, even beneath the brocade mask that sheltered her identity. She had full lips and thick dark hair spun up in a simple Greek style that framed her face perfectly.

He hadn't been thinking of how beautiful she was when he approached. In truth, he hadn't been able to see her, only the lout who was holding her, demanding what she clearly didn't want to give.

But now...now he found himself feeling things he hadn't for years. Wanting things he'd determined he would not seek during his night at the Donville Masquerade.

He shook his head. Robert was rubbing off on him.

"Does that often happen here?" he asked.

A flush of color filled her pale cheeks, but she shook her head. "No. It's never happened before. They are very careful at the masquerade. It is full agreement or nothing at all."

He pursed his lips. She spoke as though she was very experienced in what happened here. That implied she might be a lightskirt, though he couldn't believe that was true. There was an innocence about this woman. Her very proper accent and her careful choice of words said *lady* to him. Perhaps she was a bored wife or a wild heiress.

"I suppose this Rivers fellow must keep rules in place or risk no ladies coming at all for fear of being accosted," he continued. In truth, he didn't really care about the club, for he had no intention of joining. But he didn't want to step away, and that meant he had to keep talking.

She was watching him, her gaze unreadable. "Does that mean you are a new member, sir?"

"I came with my friends," he said, motioning toward the door. When he turned he found that Robert was gone and Hugh stood talking to a curvy redhead who seemed very focused on tracing the line of his jaw with her fingernail.

He cleared his throat. "Apparently they have found their desires, though."

"And what about you?" she asked. "What is your desire?"

He swallowed. "Well..."

She shook her head. "I'm sorry, I don't know what came over me. That was a terribly forward question and I shouldn't have asked it. I-I—"

She looked ready to run and he reached out to gently touch her arm. "I suppose under normal circumstances it would not be proper, but here...well, isn't that what *here* is all about?"

She licked her lips and he watched her pink tongue move. How long had it been since he felt someone's mouth on him? Someone's hands on him? Too long, if the first possibility made desire spike so high in him.

"I suppose you're right," she whispered, her gaze darting out into the rowdy, writhing crowd.

All around them people were doing such wicked things, Matthew hardly knew where to look. So he followed her stare to the dancefloor. There some couples were dancing to the music like in any ball. Others ground together in a public display of desire...foreplay.

"Would you like to dance?" he found himself asking.

She gasped and her gaze returned to him. "Dance?" she repeated.

"Not...not like that," he said, shuddering as one couple began to kiss passionately. "Just dance."

She hesitated, but then she slowly nodded. "Very well. I

would be pleased to dance with you."

The words were more impactful than he wished them to be. His head spun and he took a few seconds to gather himself before he held out a hand to her. Neither was wearing gloves— this wasn't the kind of establishment where such propriety would be expected or wanted. She looked up at him, those eyes of hers wide and dark. Her fingers trembled as she set them in his palm, and he realized in that moment that she was just as set on her heels by whatever electricity crackled between them as he was.

Somehow that didn't help.

He drew in a few deep breaths as he guided her through the crowd and onto the dancefloor just as the orchestra began the next song. It was slow, a waltz meant to force its participants into each other's arms. Matthew had not danced a waltz in years. It was once Angelica's favorite, so he hadn't the heart.

Now he began to move in time to the music, guiding the lovely stranger in his arms in a circle around the floor and wondering what the hell he had gotten himself into.

Isabel couldn't breathe as her protector danced with her with such grace. His hand was warm in hers, rough; the other pressed against her hip and made her very aware of the fact that she wore no undergarments beneath her clothing. Just a thin scrap of silk separating his skin from hers, his desire from hers.

The room was spinning, and not just because of the waltz. She had come here before and just watched, but now she was swept up in the rhythm of the dance, in the sexual intensity that crackled all around them. In the man who held her so close and stared down into her eyes like she was the only woman in the room.

She didn't know what exactly was happening, but it was hypnotic and powerful, and she didn't want it to end.

"Why are you here?" he whispered, almost to himself more than to her.

She blinked, the question breaking through the hazy fog that had settled around them. "Why is anyone here?" she retorted.

He frowned and his gaze darted around them. "For sin. Did you come here for sin?"

She swallowed and then found herself jerking out a nod. "I suppose I did. I'm not supposed to see what I see here, not supposed to feel how I feel. And yet I...I..."

She broke off and lost her footing a fraction. He steadied her by tightening his fingers on her hip, and yet that did nothing to ground her. Her body just felt like it caught on fire, her legs trembling and the apex of her thighs throbbing.

She'd felt like this before, of course. Long ago in her marriage, and now in her bed alone after nights here when she brought herself to completion.

But never so intensely.

"You like it," he said softly.

She glanced up at him. "That's wrong, I suppose."

"I don't know what's wrong and what's right anymore, I don't think," he said. "Right now it feels very...muddled."

She caught her breath. Certainly it did that. *This* wasn't what she'd come here for, this wasn't how far she'd declared she'd go. And yet here she was, in a stranger's arms, talking about things no woman was supposed to talk about.

Or so she had been told.

"Why did *you* come?" she asked.

He blinked, like her question woke him from a dream. "I don't know. Because...because I've stayed away from my life too long. Because someone told me I needed to come back to it. To this."

There was something a little mournful in those words. Pain behind the soft, deep, hypnotic sound of his voice. She shifted a bit closer and his hands tightened on her again, like he wanted her nearer.

It was in that moment she realized they had stopped moving

on the dancefloor. They stood in the middle, couples all around them, and he was just staring down at her. She up at him. Perhaps it was the masks, the anonymity, perhaps the environment, perhaps the fact that she'd been alone for a long time and that she feared a future that would potentially keep her locked away from these feelings for the rest of her life...whatever it was, she didn't feel odd standing with him.

She felt alive. For the first time in a long time, she felt alive.

He bent his head slowly, and then those full lips she had mused about from across a crowded hall were on hers. At first he was tentative, gentle, the kind of kiss a man would give to a nervous bride. Something to ease and comfort.

But then heat took over, desire took over. He drew her closer and his mouth opened. She did the same and then he was inside, his tongue probing hers with deft, powerful precision. He tasted faintly of scotch, of mint, of potent male desire.

She lifted into all of it, clutching his lapels as his fingers tightened even further on her hip and pulled her flush against him.

She was drowning and she didn't care. She'd come to watch, but this was better. This joining of mouths, this clashing of tongues...she wanted more of it. She wanted more of everything and she didn't give a damn about the consequences.

They were jostled by a drunken couple flitting by, and the stranger broke his mouth from hers. The spell was broken with it. She stared up at him, still mesmerized by his handsomeness, his command, by whatever had wrapped itself around her and made her drop every barrier she'd had in her life.

If she didn't stop now, if she didn't walk away, she would give herself to him. A stranger, a man she had no idea about. And while that thrilled her, it also terrified her. The water was too deep and she realized she was out of control.

"I-I'm sorry," she stammered, then turned on her heel and ran.

It had been an hour since the beautiful masked stranger had fled the masquerade, and yet Matthew's hands still shook as he rested them on the terrace wall. In the shadows he heard the grunts and moans of couples in the throes of passion, but he ignored them as he stared out toward the garden below.

"There you are."

He didn't turn. He knew it was Robert intruding upon his privacy. Of course it would be. Hugh would be tactful, Robert less so. It was like Matthew was being tested.

"I've been here a while," he said, still without looking at his friend. "Seems you've been busy."

"Very," Robert said with a chuckle as he stepped up beside Matthew. He was more disheveled than he had been when they first arrived, and Matthew forced himself not to roll his eyes. Trust Robert to find his pleasure without any worries or questions or consequences.

And Matthew couldn't stop thinking about a damned kiss.

"Who was she?" Robert asked.

Matthew jerked his gaze toward him. Robert's face was impassive. At least he'd find no judgment here.

"I didn't know you saw her," he said as a way to dodge the question. "You were already gone with your conquest."

"You just didn't see me," Robert said. "I may have found my conquest, but that doesn't mean I didn't take an interest in yours."

Matthew's hands tightened against the edge of the wall. He didn't like the idea of Robert having an *interest* in the lady he'd danced with.

"I don't know who she was," he admitted. "We didn't exchange names."

Robert drew back with a low whistle. "Anonymous. Very sensual."

"No. Yes. No." Matthew drew a hand through his hair. "I

don't know."

Robert wrinkled his brow as he turned toward Matthew. "Only you could make a stolen moment so complicated. Great God, man, so you liked a woman. A very beautiful woman, even with her face half-hidden by a mask. You forgot your melancholy for five minutes. What's the harm?"

Matthew turned away from. "Sod off and find your pleasure," he snapped, far more harshly than he meant. Perhaps more than Robert deserved.

But his friend was undeterred. He clapped Matthew on the back. "I love you. That may be the drinks talking, but I do. You're my brother, just like all the rest of them. It's proven by the way you put up with me despite your disapproval."

Matthew looked at him. Beneath the jovial mask, beneath the slightly drunken sway, Robert was serious. "I don't—" he began, then stopped himself. "Very well, I suppose I *do* disapprove of you sometimes. But more for your own good than what I fear you do to others. And I care for you too."

Robert smiled. "I just don't want to see you drown in misery forever."

Matthew bent his head. "I know. I know."

"If a moment with this lady you danced with, you kissed—"

"You *were* watching," Matthew breathed.

"Of course. I thought I might have to extend my backroom privileges to you and I was ecstatic." Robert shrugged. "Mostly because I hoped that you might find a little light if you gave in."

Matthew sighed. "To be honest, there was light. I have not been drawn to a woman like that since…since Angelica. It was unexpected and powerful, and I think had she not run I might have done exactly as you hoped. So perhaps you are right not to give up on me."

"I'd never give up on you," Robert said. "Now come on, I'll go introduce you to Marcus Rivers."

Matthew followed as his friend took him back inside. "The owner?" he asked. "Why?"

"So you can interview for a membership, of course," Robert tossed back over his shoulder as he moved toward the back corner of the room and a man stationed at the foot of a set of stairs.

Matthew couldn't help but laugh. "You are persistent."

"I must be. I'm the only one of our group with any sense at all," Robert said as he stopped in front of the man at the stairs. "We'd like to see Mr. Rivers, to inquire about membership for my friend."

The young man bobbed his head and disappeared up the stairs. Matthew knew he should put a stop to this, but he didn't. In the end, perhaps Robert really was right. Maybe it was time to go toward the light.

And maybe if he came here regularly, he'd bump into the lady he'd met earlier. The one who'd reminded him that there was light left in this world after all.

CHAPTER THREE

Isabel sat at the table in her uncle's breakfast room, but she hadn't touched the plate of eggs and sausage placed before her. She couldn't do it—her stomach was still aflutter from last night.

From what she'd done on a public dancefloor with a stranger, a man who had no name and only half a face. It was entirely wanton and wrong.

And she desperately wanted to do it all again.

"Eat," her uncle snapped, and she jumped at the sudden sharpness of his tone.

"I could suggest the same to you, Uncle Fenton," she said carefully, using the first words they'd spoken to each other that morning to gauge his moods.

That was always the worst part of her day, when she didn't know what his emotions were. Fenton Winter could be kind and gentlemanly, talking to her of books or music or old family stories that made them both smile. Or he could be withdrawn and dark, drowning in a grief that had pulled him under over and over again for three long, desperate years.

He smashed the paper he'd been reading down on the table, and she flinched. A bad mood, it seemed, if his dark expression was any indication.

"Something in the paper trouble you?" she asked softly as she speared her eggs and began to eat them. They tasted like nothing at all in her current state.

"Society is agog over that bastard Tyndale, that is all." Her uncle slammed a fist against the table, and the dishes shivered with the force of his anger. "The paper goes on and on about him, what an eligible bachelor he is."

Isabel took a sip of tea and took the moment both to gather herself and to observe her uncle. He was a riddle. He could be so decent, so loving. He'd been kind to her as a child and that kindness had extended to her after the death of her husband, when she'd been left with so little. Uncle Fenton had taken her in without hesitation and provided a small allowance that kept her from scraping and begging.

But beneath that kindness lurked something more. His grief. His anger. His hatred for the Duke of Tyndale, the man he currently railed against.

No amount of time had eased that.

"I understand what it is like to lose someone you…you care for," she began carefully.

He turned on her with a shake of his head. "You do not. At least your husband wasn't murdered like my Angelica."

She flinched. On his worse days, Uncle Fenton did this. Railed about how his daughter, her cousin, had been murdered. Drowned on purpose, rather than in the accident, as the world believed. And he blamed Angelica's fiancé. He blamed Tyndale.

As for Isabel, she didn't know what to believe. Men of power certainly had the means to cover up a crime they'd committed. Tyndale had much of that. His presentation to the world that he was a man deep in grieving could all be a cover, meant to thrust attention elsewhere.

She didn't know the truth. And she didn't know how to help her uncle when what he believed crippled him in throes of anger and rage like it did this morning.

"No," she said, hoping to soothe with her tone. "Gregory was taken by illness, something that plagued him during our entire marriage." Those words tasted bitter, but she ignored her own feelings for the moment. "You are correct that I cannot understand what you—what you believe happened to Angelica."

He turned his face and stared out the window. "There is no

justice. He gets to go on, living his life, adored by his ilk, while she is buried in the ground."

She dipped her head. "I'm so sorry, uncle."

"I know you are. I shouldn't have been sharp with you." He was silent for a long time, lost in thoughts. "If only I could prove it," he murmured, more to himself than to her. "If only I could destroy him like he destroyed me."

She sighed. And there was the rest of the ever-repeating cycle in her uncle's broken heart and mind. His quest for some kind of revenge. That frightened her more than anything.

"I wish I could help you," she whispered, meaning more that she wished she could help him overcome these demons, rather than find the truth he so believed was out there.

He shrugged, and then the venom left his tone as he said, "I'm just an old man talking," he muttered. "Talking too much, as always. I know it isn't fair to you." He looked at her, and his gaze had cleared a bit. "It would be better for you if you didn't have to see this, I know. We need to find you a husband, Isabel. A new husband so you can go on with your life."

She forced a smile as he went back to eating, but inside her anxiety spiked. This was another thing Uncle Fenton was determined about. Increasingly so, it seemed. He perhaps thought it a way to save her.

But she knew what a trap it would be.

"Mrs. Hayes?"

She turned to look at her uncle's butler, who was now standing at the breakfast room door. "Yes, Hicks, what is it?"

"Miss Carlton has arrived."

Isabel smiled broadly at the announcement of one of her best friends. "Thank you. Will you show her to the blue parlor?"

Hicks nodded and stepped away. When he was gone, her uncle watched as she stood. "She won't join us for breakfast, then?"

She leaned down to kiss his temple. "And bore you with our chatter about sewing and gowns and romantic novels? I would not torture you so."

He smiled, but she could see he doubted the veracity of her statement. And he had reason to, for she and Sarah very rarely talked about such mundane things. Especially recently.

She slipped down the hallway to the parlor and stepped in to see her friend standing at the window, her dark blue eyes focused on the garden behind the house. She looked troubled, and Isabel's face fell as she closed the door behind her.

Sarah turned and the trouble faded a fraction. "Isabel," she said, coming forward to take both of her friend's hands. They exchanged a kiss on the cheek before Isabel led her to the settee.

"Do you want anything? I would not recommend breaking bread with my uncle at present, but I could ask Hicks to bring us something."

"Oh, no, thank you. I ate at home with Mother." Sarah's voice caught, and Isabel leaned forward to take her hand. Sarah gave her a grateful look for the silent support. "I'm sorry. It is just that she is…not improving."

Isabel shook her head. "Oh dearest, I'm so sorry. Is there anything I can do?"

"No," Sarah whispered. "I swear it is as though the last two years have been a punishment for some unknown crime. My father's death, our financial fall, and now my mother's illness? There is nothing anyone can do, I fear."

"I can listen," Isabel said. "That is what we do for each other, isn't it? Listen. And understand."

Sarah wiped away the tears that had gathered in her eyes and forced a shaky smile. "Indeed, we do. I am so very lucky to have a friend like you. I do not mistake that fact, I hope you know it."

"I feel the same way," Isabel said.

Sarah laughed. "Well, I think the best thing for me at present would be not to talk about my situation. When I think about it, I am almost overcome with sadness and terror. Let's talk about you! Your adventures are all that buoy me in these times of trouble."

Isabel blushed. The only other person in her world who

knew her secret was Sarah. She'd never been more terrified or relieved of that fact today.

"I have adventures to share, as well," she said, sinking onto the settee. Sarah followed her, her face suddenly concerned.

"You know I worry about you in that...that place," Sarah breathed, glancing toward the door as if all the chaperones in the empire were about to come crashing down around them.

Isabel nodded. Sarah was an innocent, of course. She didn't really understand Isabel's drive to explore the passions that boiled inside of her.

"I know," she said. "I know and I won't say you don't have reasons. The Donville Masquerade is not a place for a gentlewoman."

"And yet you still go," Sarah said, worrying a loose thread on the hem of her sleeve. "I assume you went last night."

"I did. And I must tell you what happened, for I am about to burst from it."

When Sarah caught her hands and let out a shuddering sigh, Isabel took a deep breath and told her everything. From the moment when she was accosted until she'd fled from the powerful, passionate kiss of a masked stranger. When she was finished, Sarah got to her feet and paced away.

Isabel stared at her friend's back, hoping she'd not gone so far as to push Sarah away at last. But then she turned and Sarah's cheeks were bright with color. "I know I shouldn't say it, but that sounds very romantic."

Isabel bent her head. Her feelings on the matter were not exactly *romantic*. More scandalous. Wanton.

And yet the kiss *had* been rather romantic, when she retraced the steps of it. Being swept away like that, in a place where anyone could see...there was a romance to it.

"I did like it," she admitted with heat burning her cheeks. "Oh Sarah, I convinced myself I could just watch, that it would be enough, but when that man touched me...I wanted more. What is wrong with me?"

Sarah ducked her head. "Perhaps nothing. After all, there

are times I want more. Want to experience what I fear I will never have a chance to feel. And I assume your uncle continues to talk to you about remarrying."

"Nearly every day." Isabel let her breath out in a long sigh. "I know he doesn't mean to be cruel, even when he cannot help but be blunt and dark with his grief. Still, he wants to marry me off, get me out of this house so he can continue to worship at the shrine of his dead daughter. He has no intention of matching me with someone who will warm my heart. He will find me someone suitable, just like my parents did with Gregory."

Sarah worried her lip. "Right now, I would take an older merchant with money."

Isabel recoiled. "Oh, Sarah, I'm sorry. I must sound so glib and terrible considering your situation."

Sarah moved to her and took her place again. Her expression was gentle as she said, "You don't. You and I are in very different positions, that is all. There is nothing wrong with wanting someone who makes your heart sing, makes your body...weak. That is natural, I think, no matter what they tell us. I only worry that your uncle's insistence makes you...reckless."

Isabel drew in a few breaths. What she had done, what she *was* doing, it was reckless. "I'm going back," she whispered.

Sarah's eyes widened. "Isabel..."

"I know. I know it's foolish," Isabel said. "But it's now a draw I can't deny."

"And if this man is there again?" Sarah demanded. "Are you certain you will not go too far when it comes to him? Push past even more of the boundaries that you established when you first decided to do something so wild?"

Isabel leaned back and easily conjured an image of her very handsome stranger. Of his mouth on hers, his hands on her, his passion that had begun as muted and careful as her own and then flared like a wildfire.

"I don't know," she admitted. "I don't know what I will do if he is there again. I suppose it is something I will decide in the moment. I will have plenty of time to be staid and proper and alone if my uncle succeeds in his plot for my future."

Sarah nodded slowly, and for a while they sat in silence, both pondering the unfairness of the futures they each faced. Only Isabel's mind didn't stray to whatever marriage would come, but rather what would happen the next time that stranger came into her proximity.

What she would do to capture that moment of desire and connection between them.

Why was he here?

That was the question that had been in Matthew's mind from the moment he entered the Donville Masquerade for the third time in as many nights. And yet he still came, despite the little voice in his head that kept screaming at him that it was wrong.

The voice that told him Robert would laugh and laugh if he knew Matthew's desperate search for a woman whose name he didn't know, but whose taste still lingered on his lips and in his heated dreams.

"Christ," he muttered. He should just leave. He hadn't seen the lady since that first night. No one else sparked even an interest in him, despite the copious offers he'd received for scandalous acts of pleasure.

"Sir."

He turned and found the owner of the establishment had come to stand with him along the wall. Marcus Rivers was a giant of a man, almost as big as Matthew's cousin Ewan, who was the largest of their group. He was thick with muscle and one of the few not wearing a mask.

Of course, he didn't need one.

"Mr. Rivers," Matthew said, extending a hand. He'd met Rivers the night he got his membership, and though their interaction had been brief, he'd liked the man. He was shrewd and focused, driven. Matthew appreciated that in a person.

"It's nice to see you again," Rivers said, careful not to address Matthew by a title so his true identity wouldn't be exposed. He'd decided to go by a simple fabricated name, Mr. Wallace—a tip of the hat to his name, without revealing it.

"Thank you," he said, staring back out at the raucous crowd. "It's a busy night."

Rivers glanced at the crowd with a shrug. "It's always busy. People come, they get what they want, they stagger out." He wrinkled his brow at Matthew. "Except you."

Matthew shifted. "Me? What do you mean?"

"You've come here for three nights. You stand at my wall, you do not drink, you do not gamble, you do not…partake." He smiled knowingly. "You're waiting. I only wonder what for."

Matthew blinked in shock at this man, this stranger who could apparently see so clearly. "I'm surprised you put so much thought into one patron."

Rivers shrugged. "It's my job. I'm always watching. So if there is something you need, how can I help you find it?"

Matthew backed up a step. "Nothing, there is nothing that I—"

He broke off, for in that moment he saw the masked woman over Rivers' shoulder. She walked into the room, her slender hand reaching up to touch her mask reflexively. Matthew lost the ability to speak, to think, even to breathe as he gawked at her.

Rivers looked behind himself and laughed. "Ah, I see. Well, I shall leave you to it, then. Good evening."

Matthew muttered something—he wasn't even certain it was a coherent word—and moved past Rivers toward the siren he'd been dreaming about for days.

The siren he could not resist for even a moment more.

CHAPTER FOUR

Isabel was aware of the masked man coming toward her from the moment she stepped into the main hall of the masquerade. She'd found him the second she let her eyes sweep the place, almost as if she were drawn to him like a beacon. Still, she tried to remain calm as he elbowed his way through the crowd in a focused line to her.

To *her*.

Oh, but her heart was pounding as if it would burst. When he reached her side, she feared he could hear it above all the other din.

"You ran away," he said, without any preamble. As if they were picking up from the very moment they parted three nights before.

She swallowed hard. "I—yes," she admitted, shocked by how shaky her tone of voice was. She was struggling to even find the barest breath now.

He must have sensed it, for he reached out and caught her elbow, his warm fingers all but searing her sensitive flesh. "Are you quite well?" he asked, his voice low and rough. "You've gone pale."

"I am, I just…I am…"

"Would you like to get some air?" he suggested.

She found herself nodding, though that wasn't at all what she wanted. Still, it could do her good, clear her head, at least. Right now she seemed to need a clear head.

He drew her through the crowd, dodging the writhing couples and the rowdy gamblers with the precision of a man who came here all the time. Now she wondered if he did. She'd thought him a newcomer when she first saw him, but it was possible he wasn't.

It was possible he played this same game with a dozen other willing women that he was now playing with her. She didn't like that idea, even though that was the point of the Donville Masquerade after all.

To pursue pleasure.

He opened the terrace doors and led her onto the wide stone parapet. She sucked in long breaths of cool night air as she walked away from him and stood at the edge, gripping her hands against the low wall. He moved up beside her and for a moment they were quiet.

The air around them was not. Off in a dark corner, there were muffled sounds of heavy breathing, of soft sighs, and Isabel blushed as she glanced up at him. It was clear he was just as aware of the others outside with them. And what they were doing. His jaw tightened and he shifted uncomfortably.

"Have you come here often?" she asked, searching for something to say so that she wouldn't be distracted wondering what the other couple was doing to each other in the dark.

Wishing it was her and the man before her.

He shook his head. "No, I told you before the first night you saw me was my first night here," he said. "What about you?"

The heat in her cheeks flared hotter. "I-I've come before," she admitted. "Not very often, but a few times before tonight. I have a membership."

His eyebrows lifted. "I see. So the ladies are charged for their patronage, as well?"

"Less than the men, I think," she said. "But yes. I inherited a very little sum, so I took it from that."

"Inherited," he said softly. "From your father, your brother…your husband?"

She shifted and turned away from him. He was asking her

for personal details about her life. Things she should not share if she hoped to remain anonymous. And yet where was the harm, if she was careful? Talking to this man made the heat between them a little less disconcerting.

"My husband," she whispered. "He died a year and a half ago."

Something in the man next to her shifted. His demeanor changed, his hands tightened at his sides, his eyes grew faraway and filled with a riot of emotions. At last he said, "I am sorry for your loss."

"Thank you," she whispered. "It was an arranged marriage. He was much older than I was and—and it isn't as if I wanted him to die, but I suppose I should have felt more when he did." She hesitated a moment, and then what she had said sank in. She glanced up at him. "I don't know why I'd say such a thing. I don't even know you."

He shrugged. "It's the moonlight," he said softly. "It's the fact that we're wearing masks and whatever we say cannot be held against us. It brings out the truth, that little lie."

She pondered those words for a moment and then nodded. "You're probably right. The secret is the key to the truth."

"So what were you looking for in coming here?" he asked, moving a bit closer. Close enough that his warmth teased her. Beckoned her.

"I—" She bent her head. "I can't say it out loud."

"Yes you can," he insisted. He touched her chin, and he lifted it so that she was looking up into his face. His fingers spread across her jaw, brushing her cheek, and she was lost in a sea of gray.

"I just wanted to watch," she choked out at last, mesmerized by him. "Watch...*them*."

He jerked his head toward the corner of the terrace where the moans of their companions were becoming louder and more insistent. "Them?" he repeated.

She nodded. "Yes. Until you, I'd never even talked to another person at the masquerade. Certainly I'd never danced with anyone or kissed anyone. I didn't expect such a thing."

"Neither did I," he mused. "To be honest, I didn't want to come here the first night. My friend insisted and he is hard to deny. But I expected I'd stand along a wall and just be uncomfortable while I waited for him to do whatever he does here. And then there was you."

"So what you are saying is that we are two people who don't belong here and yet when we entered each other's orbit we...do?"

His fingers slid higher, into her hair, against her scalp, and she almost moaned like the woman in the corner was doing. This was an intimate touch and it woke deeper desires than to merely watch ever had.

He dropped his head, so slowly that it felt like time itself had stopped. Then his mouth was on her again, like it had been three nights ago. This time she wasn't as surprised and she lifted on her tiptoes immediately, winding her arms around his neck and opening for him to deepen this kiss.

He whispered something against her lips as he did so. A word, but she was too addled to recognize what it was. Especially when his tongue swept over hers and her entire body went liquid and ready for what would come next.

He dragged her closer, molding her body to his, letting her feel the hard planes of him against the softness of her. And there was a great deal of hardness. He was tall and lean, but muscled, strong. And she was lost to his taste and his touch and his smell in that moment.

At last he drew away, but he kept her in his arms as he stared down at her. His breath was as short as her own, his body shaking like hers.

"Does it feel like we belong?" he whispered.

She nodded, for she could form no words. She could hardly remember words.

"Will you come to a private room with...with me?" he asked, his tone hesitant.

She drew in her breath through her nose. That question was

shocking and there was a part of her that was, indeed, shocked. A deeper part, though, felt something else. A longing that she'd denied herself, even when she watched. A need that now screamed inside her head.

"Yes," she said, without meaning to do so. And yet once she had whispered it, there was no regret for having said it.

She wanted to go with him. She wanted what would happen next.

He took her hand and guided her back inside. They went to the hallway where she'd watched dozens of couples disappear over the nights she'd come here. Her masked stranger said something to the guard there, who nodded and handed over a key.

The hallway felt impossibly long as they walked down it. Behind the other doors there were the unmistakable sounds of passion. She shivered to think her own voice would soon join that chorus.

At the door, he turned the key and stepped aside to allow her to enter. She gasped. She hadn't spent an inordinate amount of time imagining these rooms, to do so was to go too far. When she had, her mind had created something tawdry. Something dirty and small.

This was not that. It was a beautiful chamber, with fine furniture, a roaring fire and lovely, if naughty, artwork decorating the walls. Images of men and women, wound together in pleasure. Mouths and hands roving like they did outer rooms. She turned her face and looked at the large bed that was the chamber's centerpiece.

He shut the door. It sounded like a shotgun blast. She jumped and then shuddered as she stared at that bed. Pictured what would happen there next. It felt almost impossible to put herself into the place of the fantasies she'd spun.

"If you want to change your mind—" he began.

She pivoted to face him and found he was leaning on the door, just watching her. She swallowed hard. This was a chance she was taking, something entirely against her character.

And yet she felt nothing but desire to do it. Her uncle was certain to match her sooner rather than later. Another old man as her husband had been, another unfulfilled life where she reached out for connection and passion and found nothing in return.

She had *earned* this night after so many empty ones. And she would hold it close to her when it was over as some reminder than she could inspire desire in a man like this.

"I realize it's wanton and even…wrong, but I *do* want this," she said with a blush. "I don't understand it, I can't explain it, but the moment I saw you it was as if this was meant to be. I don't want to change my mind."

He stared at her a beat, then pushed off the door and came toward her in three long steps. He caught her arms and kissed her again. But this time there was nothing gentle to it, nothing hesitant. He claimed, angling his head so he could drive his tongue into her mouth and taste every inch of her.

She jolted against him as sensation cascaded through her. Warmth and desire. Pleasure and anticipation. But mostly need. Hard, heavy, harsh need that throbbed between her legs and tingled through the rest of her.

She'd felt need before. That remembered need was why she'd come here in the first place. But it had never been like this. It had always been an echo—this was a symphony. Loud and riotous and utterly beautiful as it lifted her body and quieted her rowdy mind.

Her stranger's hands fisted against her back and he groaned deep in his throat as he kissed her with growing intensity. She was drowning in him, lost entirely, unable to do anything but hold tight and be swept away.

"You've done this before?" he asked, breaking from the kiss at last, though his face remained close to hers, his breath still stirred her lips and made her dizzy. "I don't want to hurt you, to compromise you."

She managed to jerk out a nod. "I have. I was married, remember?"

His gaze narrowed slightly, a troubled expression she

couldn't place. But then he dropped his mouth again and any thoughts or concerns she had regarding his reaction were gone. And it was perfect. That kiss deepened, slowed, and now it was an exploration of her. She found herself melting, her legs shaking as he continued to just kiss her.

It was amazing, unlike anything she'd ever felt before. But she wanted more. This was her only chance to get more. She had to take it, it seemed.

Her hands were flat against his chest and she slid them down to find the buttons on his waistcoat. It was a fine garment—the man was obviously very rich—and she struggled a moment to get the perfectly fitted piece open so she could push it and his jacket away.

He froze as her hands slid against the thin shirt beneath. He drew back and looked at her again. His expression was serious, thoughtful, filled with anticipation, but also hesitation.

"*You've* done this before, haven't you?" she teased gently.

The corner of his mouth quirked into a small smile, something wicked, and her stomach flipped at the sight. Even with half his face covered, this man was wildly attractive. Not the kind of man she'd ever expected to be attracted to her.

But it was the place and the masks and the moonlight, perhaps. Whatever it was, she was going to make the most of it.

"I have," he said softly, then put a little space between them and helped her get the jacket and waistcoat off. He reached up and loosened his cravat, unwinding the fabric over and over until he tossed it aside with the rest.

She caught her breath as his shirt parted and revealed just the beginnings of a well-formed chest. She swallowed hard. Her husband had been soft, older, not hideous but by no means *this*. Was she in over her head?

"Changing your mind?" he asked.

She pushed aside the hesitation. "No," she said firmly.

"Good," he whispered, and caught her shoulders. He held her stare a moment, and slowly turned her around so that her back was to him. At first she wasn't entirely sure what he was doing, not until his fingers brushed her neck, pushing away the strands of hair that had come loose from her chignon during the night. His breath was warm on her skin and then his lips were there, gentle, soft.

She shuddered with pleasure, gasped with surprise as those hands moved away from her skin and down to the top button of her gown.

He slid it free carefully and parted the fabric. She blushed as he repeated that same action over and over. She wasn't wearing undergarments. That had been her other rebellion when she came here. And as he opened the gown fully, he recognized that fact and let out a little mutter of a word she didn't recognize.

Likely he thought her a whore, but what did it matter? They were strangers, this was a stolen night. She pushed aside her embarrassment and faced him.

Her dress drooped a fraction in front and she held a hand up to hold it here. He was staring at her. Just staring, and she smiled at how wide his eyes were.

"Are *you* changing your mind?" she asked.

He shook his head. "That was the furthest thought from my mind, I assure you."

His hand trembled as he reached for her, caught her fingers, drew them away from the gown. He looped his fingers into the edge, and then he pulled. It rolled forward, the short, puffed sleeves sliding down her arms, and then she was bare from the waist up.

She felt the heat in her cheeks as he looked at her. Her husband had done this...two or three times at most in the years of their marriage? Usually when he'd touched her it had been a flip of her nightgown, a handful of grunts, and then he was finished. If he was drunk he might touch her a little, but she'd never found real pleasure with him. Only with her own hand.

And now this stranger was staring at her naked breasts. The ones that were too small, according to her husband. Too pink. Too...well, whatever *too* came to his cold lips at the time.

"Beautiful," he breathed and she jerked her gaze to his face.

He wasn't teasing or taunting.

She pushed the sleeves from her arms and the dress folded around her waist, sliding low on her hips. It was precariously close to falling and leaving her entirely naked, but she didn't focus on that.

She wanted to see him, too.

She stepped a fraction closer and unfastened the first button on his shirt. Her hands were shaking so hard, she could hardly get it open.

"Here," he said, pulling it from his waist before he popped open a few of the buttons and tugged the entire thing over his head. His mask was cockeyed when he removed it, and he adjusted it back to its place before he tossed the shirt aside.

And she stared, her breath gone. What was before her was utter male perfection. His body was lean and muscled, his chest hard as granite, with a peppering of chest hair that narrowed into a line that disappeared into the waist of his trousers.

She couldn't help herself. She reached out and laid her hand on his skin. He grunted and she sighed. He was hot and real— *this* was real. She slid her hand across him, tracing the muscles she found, reveling in hard muscle under softer skin. In that wild moment, she wanted to lick him and touch him and do everything and anything she'd ever seen in the open rooms of the hall.

She wanted to be wanton for him. Wild.

It seemed he wanted the same, for he suddenly caught the gown still around her waist and tugged her against him. Her breasts flattened against the wall of his chest and his mouth hit hers in hungry possession and need. She rubbed against him, her nipples growing hard at the abrasion of his chest.

She was being lifted then. He marched her to the bed and set her down there. They never stopped kissing even as he pushed the rest of her gown away. She kicked at her slippers, and he lifted her to the bed and set her there.

She settled blindly against the pillows as he at last stepped back. She was naked and he was staring at her, his hungry gaze gliding from top to bottom, like he was memorizing her. Like was planning a move against another country.

Then he tugged his boots off and stripped his trousers away, leaving him as naked as she was. She sat up on her elbows to get a better look. Great God, he was perfect everywhere. His hips were trim, his legs muscled and his cock already hard and curling toward his belly.

He leaned over her on the bed, caging her in as he settled over her. She felt the length of him nudge her stomach, and she jolted at how hard he was. How hot and thick and ready. On instinct, she parted her legs, lifting to meet him.

He glanced at her in surprise. "We're not halfway to that yet," he whispered.

She blinked with confusion. They were naked on a bed. That was more than she'd usually experienced in this act. She was already wet, she was tingling in anticipation. The next step was for him to join that exquisite body with her own, and then it would be over and burned into her memory forever.

"You look surprised," he said as he pressed a kiss to her neck.

"I am," she admitted.

He lifted his stare to hers. "Some husband he was," he whispered. "Let me show you."

His mouth glided over her skin, his tongue just barely tasting as he moved down the column of her neck, traced her collarbone, then lower. He leaned back a fraction and watched as he covered her breasts with his hands. She arched as unexpected sensation rushed through her. It intensified as he began to stroke his fingers against her, brushing his thumbs against her nipples until her breath left her.

And then he dropped his mouth to one breast and traced her nipple with his tongue. She'd seen men in the halls do this with their lovers, but she'd never felt it. Now she let out a cry in the quiet of the room. The wet heat of his mouth against her already ultrasensitive nipple was too much. Too much sensation. It shot through her body and she arched against the flow of it.

He smiled against her body—and then he sucked. She jolted with the feel of it, the surprising burst of pleasure. It was perfect, not too hard, not enough to create pain, but just enough to wake up every part of her she hadn't realized was asleep. She heard herself moaning, sighing, rather like the women in the club did so many nights.

And she surrendered to it all as he moved to her opposite breast and repeated his actions, all the while massaging the one he had left behind. She lifted her hips as he did so, reveling in the warmth and heat that flooded her, the desire that built ever higher with each unexpected touch. When he at last released her nipple with a pop and looked up her body, she braced again. Her body was most certainly ready for him now. She felt like she was on fire.

And yet he still didn't rear up over her and mount her. His lips glided lower, to her stomach. His hands skimmed her hips, tracing the line of her body, cupping her backside and lifting her. Her legs fell open and she stared as he settled between then, his face even with her sex.

Her cheeks were on fire now. This was far too intimate, far too wild. Something women in this club did, but not ladies. Certainly ladies did not—

The thought was cut off when he touched her sex, gently parting the folds and revealing her fully. She was shaking as he blew a gust of hot breath to her most hidden secret places. Her husband had never done this. She'd seen men do it but never pictured herself on the receiving end.

He licked her.

She gripped the sheets in both hands and gasped as her body lifted of its own accord. He licked her again and her heels dug into the mattress. Then she could no longer distinguish one lick from the next. His tongue moved over her, around her, inside of her, tasting and teasing. Tempting and tormenting. She turned her head against the pillow with a shuddering sigh. She lifted her hips, grinding into his mouth, surrendering to the unexpected and powerful pleasure he was creating with every movement.

Every lick, *everything*.

She had touched herself before. Found that slick nub that made her body quake with intense waves of pleasure. He found it too, and suddenly the focus on his tongue switched to that sensitive place. He laved it, he swirled around it, he sucked it. She felt herself building to the release she'd found with her hands, but it felt different this time. More powerful, certainly more out of control. She reached for it desperately, wanting it more than breath or life in this moment.

And then it was there. She let out a keening cry she knew would echo in the hall. She didn't care. Waves of sensation were washing over her, her hips jerking against them, against him and the intensity he was creating. She wanted more, she needed less, she wanted everything.

And he continued on, tormenting her through the crisis until she flopped weak and spent on the pillows. She felt him move, his mouth retracing the path back up her body. She glided her fingers into his hair, murmuring pleasure as he licked and nibbled his way over every crest and valley of her body. He reached her mouth and she opened to him, tasting the earthy flavor of her own body on his tongue as he drove it deep inside her mouth.

She sank into the sensation once more, her body still throbbing from release. It was nothing like she'd ever felt, not on her own, certainly not with her husband.

The stranger nudged her knees a bit wider and she allowed it, spreading herself like a wanton beneath him. There was the press of him at her entrance and she broke away from the kiss with a gasp as he settled against her, breaching her just the tiniest bit with the hard thrust of his cock.

"Change your mind?" he murmured, his voice thick with desire.

Her gaze flitted to his face. "It's a little late for that," she managed to gasp out.

He shook his head. "It's never too late to say no."

She stared at him. There was nothing false about the look

in his eyes. If she refused him, he would pull away and that would be the end of it. He would let her have her pleasure and walk away without any other demands.

"I don't want to say no," she said softly. "But it's been a long time."

A tiny smile quirked up one side of his mouth, and then he said, "For me too."

He thrust gently as he said it and then he was inside, really inside. Her body stretched to welcome him, then more of him. She let out a long sigh as he took more and more. It felt so damned good, so right as he fully seated himself inside of her and rested his forehead to hers with a ragged breath.

For a moment, he just lay like that, their bodies entangled, their breath matching. But then he ground his hips and the quiet connection dissolved into something far more animal and passionate.

He took. Like a man possessed, he thrust, circling his hips with every down stroke, teasing her with every withdrawal. She rose to meet him, clawing at his back as the pleasure she'd felt moments ago mounted once more. She had no idea if she could find more than one release, but she reached for it regardless, mewling out wordless sounds as sensation shot through every nerve in her body.

She lifted as he swiveled those trim hips and the orgasm came again. This time it was more intense, and she clung to him helplessly as he drove her through the waves harder and faster. She shivered beneath him, swept away from thought and reason and everything but the powerful sensation of surrendering all she was to this man she didn't even know.

If anything, that made it even more powerful.

"I can't wait," he gasped, that deep voice lined with strain.

"Don't wait," she cried out.

He withdrew as her body continued to flutter with release, and roared out a desperate sound of pleasure. He pumped his cock and came before he flopped down beside her on the bed, taking great gulps of air like he'd run from London to Brighton.

THE DUKE OF HEARTS

She reached out and curled her hand against his chest, almost to make sure this was real. It had actually happened.

Because it felt like a dream. And she didn't want to wake up.

CHAPTER FIVE

Matthew flopped an arm over his eyes as he struggled to regain his breath. He'd never intended for this to happen when he came to the club with Robert and Hugh a few nights before. If either of them had suggested such an outcome, he would have told them they were crazy. Uncouth.

And yet here he was, body tingling from the most powerful release he had experienced in years, this woman's sweet flavor still on his lips, and he felt...

Calm.

He flinched as that word settled into his mind. Since Angelica's death, he'd been restless and empty. Always thinking. Sometimes it felt like always remembering. And yet in those moments when he'd been lost in this other woman, he'd felt peace.

Was that a betrayal?

As he pondered that, her hand settled against his chest. He lowered his arm and looked down at that hand. Slender fingers bunched against his body. He felt the weight of each one and wanted to feel more of it. More of those hands moving over him. And when he followed the line of her arm and looked at the beautiful woman at his side, he wanted that mouth, too. He wanted to remove that intricate mask and see her entire face when she bucked in pleasure beneath him.

And *that* was a betrayal, certainly. One stolen, anonymous night could be forgiven, perhaps. This strange feeling that it wasn't enough was too much.

He sat up and caught her hand, lifting it to his lips to brush a kiss over her palm. "Thank you," he said, hoping she would understand what he meant.

She'd had a soft smile on her face, but now that faded and she swallowed hard. "Certainly," she whispered. "Thank you."

There was a strange ache in his chest as he got up and began to gather his clothing. He felt her watching him as he did so, and searched for any topic to fill the now uncomfortable space in the room between them.

"Well, you can now say you've been in the infamous back rooms of the Donville Masquerade," he said as he stepped into his trousers. "That is something."

"Not something to brag about, I suppose. At least not for a woman."

He turned and found she'd lifted the sheet to cover herself. The disappointment that flowed through him at that fact was not something he chose to ponder. "You don't regret it, do you?"

She got out of the bed, blushing as she revealed herself once more. She put her back to him as she gathered up her dress, and he caught his breath. The sight of her bent over the gown was enough to drive a man mad.

He was turning into Robert—that was all there was to it. Crazed by desire.

"I don't regret it," she said, breaking into his thoughts. "I didn't know I needed it so much until…" She trailed off and tugged her dress on. "Will you button me?"

Undressing her had been a dizzying pleasure. There was no way not to brush her skin and the same would be true now. He took his time sliding each button into place and let his fingers touch her skin. She stiffened each time he did, her breath coming shorter.

He felt the throb of desire between his legs, felt his cock slowly making its way back to attention. What the hell was wrong with him? He'd never been a randy wanderer, even before Angelica. Sex had been something he enjoyed, certainly, but he didn't recall it burning in his blood like this. Making him want to take and take until there was nothing left of him or the woman in his arms.

He just didn't understand it.

She pulled away as he fastened the last button and walked somewhat unsteadily toward a mirror affixed above the fire. She looked at herself, and occasionally her gaze flitted to him in the mirror image as she began to fix her hair.

"Do *you* regret it?" she asked.

He shook out his shirt. "No," he said softly before he tugged it over his head.

It tangled briefly around the mask he wore and he managed to get himself free. But when he smoothed the fabric down, the mask was now half-cockeyed around his cheeks. He swore beneath his breath and untied it, then removed it and brushed it off.

He heard her gasp just as he began to lift the mask back in place. He looked up to see her staring at him. Just staring, her eyes wide with what seemed to be terror and shock. Her hands trembled and her lips were parted.

"What is it?" he asked.

She shook her head. "I-I—"

She said nothing more, but ran from the room. He stared at her retreating back and then strode after her. "Wait!" he called out, but she was already running into the increasingly crowded hall. Barefoot, he'd never catch her.

He got to the end of the hall and craned his neck, but as he suspected, she was lost in the swell of grinding bodies.

With a shake of his head, he turned back to the chamber to finish fixing himself. As he did, his mind spun. She'd seen him. That was the only reason for her terror, for her quick escape.

But why? Why would she react so strongly to his face? Unless…she knew him. Or knew of him. Or he knew her. His stomach turned with the possibilities.

He sat down and began to tug on his boots. There were plenty of bored married women who came to these soirees. His stranger had told him she had once been married, that she was a widow, but that could have been a lie to hide what she currently was. She could be the wife of a friend.

Not a wife of one of his duke club. He didn't believe that for a moment. All of them were deeply in love with their husbands, and he doubted any were lacking in pleasure in their lives.

But he had friends outside that circle. Could one of their wives have strayed only to be confronted with the horror of what she'd done once she saw his face?

That was certainly one possibility. One he found himself sick about, for the idea that he would betray a friend mixed with the concept that this mystery woman who had so set him on his heels was not...free was terrible, indeed.

However, it wasn't the only possibility.

He got to his feet and shoved his shirt back into the waist of his trousers before he found his tangled waistcoat and jacket.

It could be she was a servant. Someone who knew his face because she had brought him tea or served him roast. The fact that he had touched her could get her sacked, at least in her mind. Or put into a compromising position where she did not get to choose her own path.

He wrinkled his brow at his reflection. That didn't seem correct, though. The lady he'd bedded had worn a fine gown and her hair had been done like she'd had help with it. Her hands were soft—she clearly didn't do work with them.

Still, it was a possibility.

He supposed the third option was that the woman had simply been shocked that his identity was revealed. She'd wanted an anonymous encounter and he had violated the terms of that agreement when he removed his mask for adjustment. Now she couldn't so easily push aside what they had done. Forget it, as perhaps she wished to.

He looked at his own reflection in the same mirror she had so recently examined herself in. Whatever the reason for her quick exit, he couldn't help but feel concern for her well-being.

And he found himself smiling at his reflection.

He had intended to tell the woman that this was a wonderful night, but one he should not repeat. But now…

Well, now it would be ungentlemanly not to approach her if he saw her again.

"To reassure her," he said to his reflection. "That's all."

He turned away from the liar in the mirror and made his way from the room. As he exited, a chambermaid stepped up. "Are you finished with the room, sir?"

Matthew looked off in the direction where his lady had run. Then he nodded. "For tonight, yes."

She wrinkled her brow at the strange turn of phrase, but her questioning faded when he tossed her a coin and left her there.

He would come back. Even if he'd been telling himself he shouldn't. He would come back and he would find the lady again. Just one more time. And then it would be over.

That was how it had to be.

Isabel shook as sobs racked her body. The carriage driver was unaware, of course, and drove on, turning down this street and that, knocking her around and making her very aware of the delicious soreness of her body that had been caused by *him*.

She lifted her head and wiped at the tears on her cheeks. She knew him. The magical stranger had been transformed in an instant from a gentle lover to a man she'd been told to fear for three long years. To hate. To suspect.

"How could he be Matthew Cornwallis?" she asked herself out loud. "How could he be the Duke of Tyndale?"

The tears returned and she flopped down on the carriage seat as she let them flow. Life was too cruel. It was so punishing. She had gone to the Donville Masquerade for anonymous thrills. Things to think about as she furtively touched herself in her lonely bed. Things to recall once she was married off to yet another man who would have no interest in her.

A real lover was never meant to be a part of that. Certainly not a lover who turned out to be the greatest enemy of her family.

She flashed to his mouth on her, to the gentle coaxing of deepest pleasures that she hadn't known she could feel. Her body shuddered at just the memory, and she shoved it aside.

"No!" she snapped at herself.

She could not look fondly on that night. It was wrong to do so. At the very least Tyndale had once been her late cousin's fiancé! That made what she'd done bad enough. But that her uncle believed him to be a killer?

"It's too much," she murmured as anxiety rose in her chest. "Too much."

The carriage pulled around behind her uncle's home as she had instructed and the hack driver came down to open the door for her. She handed him money and he looked her up and down. "You've been a naughty girl," he said, his tone lewd.

She glared at him, trying to behave as if his words didn't rattle her in an already rattling situation. "Mind your own affairs," she bit out, and then stepped up to the gate.

She heard him laughing as she entered the garden and then ran as fast as her legs would carry her. But she couldn't run from what she'd done. She couldn't run from how it made her feel.

CHAPTER SIX

"And to what do I owe this great pleasure so early in the morning?"

Matthew turned to watch as Robert entered the parlor, hand outstretched in welcome. His friend had a hint of shadow beneath his eyes and his hair was slightly tousled, as if he had been abed recently.

"It's noon," Matthew said with a shake of his head.

Robert shrugged one shoulder. "If you say so. I realize most people don't keep the civilized hours I do. Would you like a drink?"

"No," Matthew said, and couldn't help a laugh even though he wasn't feeling in particularly good humor today. That was what lying awake, tossing and turning, while one thought of soft sighs and intense pleasure did to a man.

And here he was. An act of desperation.

"What's wrong?" Robert asked, his teasing quality gone, replaced by concern.

Matthew flopped himself into the closest chair. "I'm not looking forward to how much you will crow."

Robert took a place on the settee and leaned forward. "Oh, this *does* sound good."

"I've been going back to the Donville Masquerade," Matthew admitted in a rush, as if he pushed all the words together that Robert wouldn't react to them.

Which, of course, was not true. His friend's eyes went

almost impossibly wide and then his grin went even wider. "Have you now? I knew even you would be seduced by the many pleasures to be found there."

Matthew sighed. "It isn't the many pleasures. I went back looking for...for that woman I met the first night."

"The one you kissed."

"Yes." Matthew found his foot tapping restlessly and forced himself to stop. "When she didn't come, there was nothing found there for me. And then, last night, she returned."

Robert lifted his eyebrows. "Pursuing one lass wasn't *exactly* what I had in mind when I encouraged you to get a membership at the club, but it's better than you roaming your estate like a ghost. So you saw the young woman and then..."

This was the difficult part. Matthew had never been one to talk about his conquests. He had no intention of going too far when he did it today, either. This was not a bragging session, but a plea for help. No matter how Robert might turn it on its head.

"What do you think happened?" he asked, his voice sharper than he had perhaps intended. But then it seemed everything in his life was currently out of control.

Robert's expression was shocked. "I'm going to hazard a guess that you bedded her." Matthew swallowed hard, and his expression seemed to give the answer Robert required. "That is good news. Isn't it? Why do you look like that? Why do you look more miserable than you did before? Quite a herculean feat, by the way."

"You must understand," Matthew began. "It's been such a long time."

"So you said," Robert said softly. "Too long to be healthy. Are you saying you were terrible at it?"

Matthew smiled at the teasing in his friend's tone. He appreciated it, actually. Robert was trying to put levity into the situation.

"I wasn't terrible at it," he said as he thought of his beautiful stranger's mewls and cries of pleasure. At the way her tight, slick body had milked his until he nearly lost control and came deep inside of her.

"Then what is the problem?" Robert asked. "Please don't tell me you are prostrating yourself on the altar of guilt and remorse just because you spent a few hours pursuing natural and healthy pleasure with a willing partner."

"When you put it that way, it makes me sound like a fool," Matthew said. "And I wouldn't say prostrating myself. It's just that...I don't know. You, of all people, would not understand."

Robert held his gaze a beat, and then he said, "You thought you had found the one person who would keep your heart for the rest of your life. Like the others have. You believed that your future was set. And then it was torn out from under you in the most cruel and terrible way possible. Worse, there are some who have blamed you for it. So you've spent all this time mourning what might have been and cursing what is. And when a young lady finally moves your...shall we say heart or cock?" He laughed. "Well, either way, I suppose it must be very disconcerting. And it must also awaken some dark and dangerous memories and feelings."

Matthew gaped at him. "I would not have expected that summary from you."

A ghost of a smile slipped over Robert's face. "I do not believe in love for myself. It does not mean I discount it for anyone else. And I'm a cad, proud as hell of it, and with no intention of ever changing, thank you, but I'm not an idiot."

"No one would ever accuse you of that," Matthew said softly. "And yes, what you say is exactly part of it. At first, I was merely mourning. Coming to terms with what had happened to Angelica and my part in it. Then more and more time passed and it was as if I became...paralyzed by my grief, regret...my anger and my disappointment."

"And then this girl popped up," Robert said. "And suddenly you were awake again. Perplexing, I would imagine."

"Quite."

"So you came here for advice on how one circumvents all deeper feeling in the pursuit of pleasure?" Robert asked. "I am the expert."

"No." Matthew chuckled. "I'm here because last night, when it was all over, she saw my face. And she ran."

Robert leaned back in the settee with a shake of his head. "My God, it's like a novel. Or a children's story with a very naughty twist. You think she recognized you?"

"It's the best explanation. She knows me somehow and it terrified her. So she ran. And I...want to find out who she is. Will you help me?"

Robert arched a brow. "Me? Why would you ask me? I'm the one who would sigh in relief if a lady ran away after making love. Makes the set down a bit easier."

"Somehow I doubt your ego would love a woman running, practically screaming from your bed," Matthew said. "And I'm asking you because Hugh is distracted, Kit is...dealing with his father's illness and everyone else is—"

"Pushy," Robert finished. "Very pushy since they married."

Matthew nodded. "That's one word for it. If I mentioned an interest in a woman, no matter how unsavory the beginning, they would start falling over each other encouraging me to marry for love like they have. One of us four must be the next, in their eyes."

Robert recoiled. "Well, it won't be me. You and I already discussed this."

"It *can't* be me," Matthew said. "I barely allowed myself to take a little pleasure last night. I'm not thinking about forever."

"And yet you want to find her," Robert said.

Matthew rolled his eyes. "Don't you start. I want to find her because her reaction troubled me. I need to know why she was so frightened when she saw my face."

"No other reason," Robert drawled.

Matthew felt heat in his cheeks. "I have no idea what you're talking about. It was one night of pleasure—I had no expectation of anything more. You of all people should know that feeling."

Robert held up his hands, almost in surrender. Then he smiled. "It is good to see you driven by something other than grief. I'll help you. Only it won't be easy. Rivers guards his membership roster jealously."

"It's in his best interest to do so, of course," Matthew said. "But does that mean there's no hope in discovering who she is?"

"I can check around, ask some questions, grease some wheels with a little blunt," Robert said.

"I don't need you to—"

"Don't you dare take away my pleasure in this little game," his friend interrupted. "I have more than enough to play. Your best bet, however, might simply be to keep going to the Donville Masquerade. She was going there before, we know at least twice."

"You think she would return after such an abrupt exit?" Matthew asked, and his heart leapt at the thought.

Robert shrugged. "I have no idea what goes on in the minds of women. But if this encounter between you was powerful enough to inspire you to chase, inspired her to run…it follows that she might return to the scene of the…*crime* might be too strong a word."

"Yes, thank you," Matthew said. "Very well. I can do that. I'll go back to the Donville and continue looking for her. And if you can find out her identity before I see her again, then all the better."

"What do you intend to do when you find her?" Robert asked.

Matthew opened and shut his mouth a few times. There was a question he'd been trying very hard not to answer, even to himself. Check on her was the first answer that rushed to his lips, but he knew that his desire went far deeper than that. Deep enough that it was not something he wished to ponder overly much.

He'd find her. And what to do would become clear then.

Isabel watched as her uncle paced in front of the portrait of Angelica. The fact that he had insisted they take their tea in this parlor, in front of the shrine he had built there to the daughter he'd lost, was not helping Isabel's nerves whatsoever.

Every time she looked at Angelica's beautiful face, she thought of Tyndale, poised between her own thighs, his wonderful tongue doing wildly pleasurable things.

She thought of that, and the moment when his mask had slipped and she'd realized that the man who had given her such pleasure was the very one Uncle Fenton had been railing on about for years. The one he believed had killed her cousin.

The one he despised more than any other man on this earth.

"Uncle?" she said, interrupting his pacing.

He jolted, almost as if he had forgotten she was there, and turned to her. He looked tired. Drawn out. He didn't sleep much, she knew that. Grief had gripped him and it sometimes felt like it was edging toward madness. But she had no idea what to do for him.

"What is it?" he asked.

She swallowed hard. To talk to him about this was to open a Pandora's box. And yet she had to do it. For her own sanity.

"Do you truly believe that Tyndale killed my cousin?" she asked.

He stiffened and his gaze grew faraway. Clouded. "She drowned," he said, the tremble heavy in his voice. "She drowned and it was his fault. He did it to her. He did it."

Isabel gripped her hands in her lap. That was not exactly a satisfactory or even clear answer. There were so little details about Angelica's death. Drowning, yes, she knew that. It had been labeled as a tragic accident by Society. People had clucked their tongues and murmured sympathetic noises at her family, at the duke, himself.

It was only Uncle Fenton who implied that Tyndale had more to do with it. That somehow he was at fault. But he never made it clear what he meant by the accusation. Isabel had never felt motivated to garner more details from him. He believed

Tyndale responsible and that had little to do with her.

Until now. Now that she had climbed into a bed with Matthew, given herself to him entirely, the facts of that horrible night seemed far more pressing. And her uncle's belief seemed far less acceptable. Tyndale had been nothing but gentle with her. Passionate, but kind.

It was hard to believe he was a killer, as Uncle Fenton did.

She tapped her foot beneath her gown and looked at Angelica's portrait. They could have been no less alike. Her cousin had been fair and tall. Isabel was dark and petite. Angelica was popular and rich, Isabel came from a merchant's family. Their only connection to Society was her uncle on her mother's side.

She'd *liked* her cousin, of course. Angelica had been a few years older and so sophisticated and beautiful. How could one not be enchanted by her?

Now she found herself looking at the portrait and wondering about her relationship with Matthew. Not just the particulars of her death, but the details of whatever life they had shared. Had Angelica kissed him as Isabel had? Had she given herself to him?

She didn't know the answers. By the time Angelica was engaged to the man, they'd been living such different lives. Isabel was just coming out in their Society, her father was already arranging her own marriage. They barely wrote anymore, and when Angelica did her letters were filled with upper Society tidbits about people Isabel didn't even know and vague references to her future.

She'd seemed happy enough, certainly, and Isabel hadn't been that interested in pressing into a world she had no connection to. Now she wished she had.

"Would you mind very much if I called on Sarah?" Isabel asked.

Her uncle ceased his pacing and stared at her. He shrugged. "Whatever you like. Take the carriage, but I need it back by six. I have an appointment."

"Certainly," Isabel said. "Thank you, uncle."

He ignored her and pivoted to look at the portrait of his daughter. She frowned. When he did that, he would sometimes get lost for hours. And drink. And God knew what else.

She slipped from the room and asked for the carriage. Soon she was dashing through the streets, her hands clenched in her lap, wondering how she was going to tell Sarah what had happened.

And wondering what in the world she would do next.

"The Duke of Tyndale?" Sarah gasped. "The one your uncle is convinced killed your cousin?"

"Yes," Isabel said, sinking into the closest seat and covering her eyes. She had been at Sarah's house for all of ten minutes and the entire story had spilled from her lips. "Oh God. I never meant to go so far with any man. But how could it be him, Sarah? How?"

"It is a mighty coincidence," her friend said, voice trembling. "But how...was it?"

Isabel stared at her with wide eyes. Sarah had never been married—she was an innocent, and yet she seemed truly interested in details of activities that Isabel knew she shouldn't talk about. But oh, how she needed to do just that.

"Wonderful. Erotic," she admitted with a deep blush. "Terrifying."

Sarah's jaw tightened in displeasure at that last descriptor. "Because he was threatening?" she asked.

Isabel shook her head. "No, not at all. He was gentle. He was even kind."

"I'm glad of that." The tension seemed to bleed from Sarah's face. "But it does beg the question of *why* you did it."

Isabel pushed to her feet and paced the room. "Because...my future is already laid out. My father ensured it.

Now my uncle intends to do the same. Neither one is worried about my heart, my body…just my financial security. It is the way of our world, but it is so…"

Sarah sighed. "Depressing. To think that there would never be…love or passion."

Isabel turned and found Sarah's head bent. She moved to her and caught her hands. "How bad is it?"

Sarah pursed her lips. "You want to change the subject and we shall, but not yet. I understand why, I do. And so do you. But what will you do?"

"I don't know," Isabel said with a shudder. "What can I do after…*this*? I don't want to believe that Tyndale is a killer. Not after last night. Honestly, not even before. But now I've…I've given myself to him and that was never in the plan to begin with. So what *do* I do?"

"Does he know who you are?" Sarah asked.

"I don't think so. My mask remained on, somehow. And even if it had come off, we never met."

"You didn't?" Sarah seemed surprised.

"You and I are from different worlds." Isabel shrugged. "I wasn't raised to go to Society parties like you were. Perhaps I could have done thanks to my mother's connection to Uncle Fenton, but my father was against it. A lower-class snob, my uncle called him."

"But still, you were family. Close enough for your uncle to take you in once your husband died and your mother and father were gone."

The look on Sarah's face told Isabel that she was thinking of her own mother, so sick in a bedroom above. Isabel clenched her friend's hands tighter in support.

"No, never met. If they had married, I would have. I was invited to the wedding. But of course Angelica died before it could happen. I just know him due to portraits and my uncle pointing him out if we passed him in a carriage or a park."

"Isn't it possible he saw a portrait of you?" Sarah suggested.

"I suppose it is. But it's doubtful. Angelica didn't carry

miniatures of me around, I assure you. If he saw one of me in my uncle's home, it would have been one done when I was a little girl. There would be no way for him to recognize me."

Sarah seemed to ponder that a moment. Then she gave Isabel a look. "Could you...could you use the opportunity to investigate him?"

Isabel drew back. She'd been so wrapped up in abject terror and confusion and heated memories of being in the man's bed, she hadn't thought of that as a possibility. "How do you mean?" she asked.

"He wanted you," Sarah said. "Enough that he gave you a wonderful and erotic night in his arms."

Isabel shuddered slightly. "You forgot terrifying. If you're going to throw my words back at me, throw them all."

"But it was terrifying because you, the planner, did not control or expect what happened, yes?" Sarah pressed.

Isabel sighed. "Yes. It was the shock of it, and of discovering his identity, that made me say terrifying."

"Well, then your running away likely only increased his desire."

Isabel wrinkled her brow. "Is that true?"

Sarah stared off toward the window for a moment, her expression pinched. "When ladies run, gentlemen follow."

Isabel's lips parted. The bitterness in her friend's tone reminded her that Sarah was more involved in the world of Matthew and his friends than she was. And it had ended badly.

"Are you thinking of the Duke and Duchess of Crestwood?" she asked. "That situation two summers ago?"

Sarah glanced at her. Isabel knew there were few people she had told that story to. That her friend had thought for a moment that Crestwood might be interested, but his passion for Meg had been too powerful, despite her engagement to his friend. The entire situation had exploded, and in a moment in her cups, Sarah had said something to Meg and been taken to task on it.

Now Sarah's cheeks were dark with embarrassed color. "They're well matched," she admitted at last. "It's obvious they deeply love each other. I just...I've lost so much since then. I think I regret the opportunity, the last one I had, rather than the man."

"I wish I could help you."

"You can't," Sarah said. "I am in the position I am in. There is nothing that can be done about it. But you are in a *different* position. You'll be taken care of, no matter what happens. So you can do things so you *don't* regret the opportunity or the man."

"Are you talking about the opportunity to, as you say, investigate Tyndale, or to have an excuse to see him again?" Isabel asked.

Sarah smiled, and some of the trouble left her gaze. "Both. One leads to the other, at any rate."

Isabel got up. "You are talking about me seducing him in order to determine if he did something to my cousin."

Sarah nodded. "It would be dangerous, I suppose."

"Except I can't believe my uncle's accusations are true," Isabel said. "After spending a little time with him, intimately at that, I don't see him as the kind of man who would do something to hurt someone he loved. To hurt anyone at all."

"You don't want to believe it," Sarah suggested.

"I don't want to believe it," Isabel repeated. "But if I could prove his innocence, wouldn't that free my uncle?"

"He is obsessed," Sarah said. "I've seen the altar he's built to Angelica, I've heard him rail in desperation about her being taken from him. If you could free him of the notion that his daughter was murdered, I would hope it would leave him to grieve and perhaps move on."

"Yes." Isabel's thoughts on the matter becoming lighter as they analyzed the benefits. "That would be a selfless reason to do something so bold."

"And you want to see him again," Sarah said, folding her arms and spearing Isabel with a look.

Now it was her turn to have her cheeks heat. "I...do. I do want to see him again. I panicked when I realized who he was, but it doesn't change that night and how it made me feel. It doesn't change that soon I will never get to feel that way again. There is no reason for him to find out it is me, is there? I still won't move in his circles. There is no harm that can come of it."

She was saying it to convince herself, not Sarah. And she was doing just that.

"It seems like a scenario with very little downside," Sarah said. "Unless he turns out to be a killer."

Isabel flinched at the thought and pushed it aside. "Well, if he does, then perhaps I could help bring him to justice. You are right. I should do this. It's my only chance."

Sarah smiled softly. "You know I know about those. You can't walk away from them."

"And I won't," Isabel said. "I won't. I'll go back to the masquerade and find him again. And this time I'll do it with my eyes wide open and my agenda in place."

"But you'll wait a few days," Sarah said.

Isabel's heart dropped far more quickly than it should have. "Why?"

"Because you're running, Isabel," Sarah laughed. "And the longer you do so, the more desperate he'll be in the chase. And in whatever happens once he catches you."

Isabel swallowed hard as she recalled his hands on her, his mouth on her, his big body moving over and in her. Desperate seemed a good thing when it came to desire.

And she was about to see what it looked like on the Duke of Tyndale.

CHAPTER SEVEN

Isabel stepped into the hall of the Donville Masquerade three nights later and her heart leapt. Everything around her suddenly felt different. More alive. More vibrant.

In her previous times coming here, she had looked, stared, felt her body react. She'd known she'd go back to her home and ease her desires with her own hand, and that would be the end of it.

Now, as she looked at the writhing bodies, the dark and desperate connections, as she scented the sex on the air, she felt something different. A deeper kinship to passion, to play, to doing things one shouldn't do, if only because of the protection of a thin mask.

It was all still titillating, but now her eyes sought something different. She wanted…wanted…

Him.

There he was, standing across the room at the bar with the Duke of Roseford. Matthew wore a mask, but he was instantly recognizable, and her heart rose to her throat as she tried to decide if she should go forward with her bold and daring plan.

Or run off into the night once more.

It was he who decided that for her. Suddenly his gaze fell on her and he straightened up, his eyes locking with hers and somehow drawing her across the room to him. Almost against her very will. He was fire and she couldn't resist jumping straight into the flame.

She could scarcely breathe by the time she reached him, and she clenched her trembling hands by her sides so that they wouldn't be too obvious as he swept his gaze over her from top to bottom.

"You're here," he breathed.

She had no opportunity to respond when his friend shouldered his way in between them and smiled at her. It was a rather dazzling smile at that—she could see why every woman in the room cooed over Roseford. She felt no desire to do so, even if she recognized his charisma and charm.

"You are, indeed, Miss Swan," he said.

She froze. That was her secret name. The one she gave to gain entry into the club each time she arrived. He shouldn't have known it.

"Y-your Grace," she said.

He laughed and elbowed Matthew. "I am. The Duke of Roseford, at your service, most especially if you bore of this one. So, you know my name. But finding out yours has been quite difficult."

She swallowed. He'd been trying to find out her name? She glanced at Matthew, whose jaw was set hard and eyes were narrowed at Roseford.

"Enough, Robert," he growled. "If the lady wishes to remain anonymous, that is her right."

"Ah yes," Robert drawled, and winked at her. "The eroticism of anonymity. I wouldn't dare disrupt that." He smiled. "I suppose I'm only curious to know more about the lady who has brought my friend back from the dead."

Isabel jolted at that choice of words, dark considering what her uncle suspected of him. When she jerked her face to Tyndale, she found his lips thin and white, his irritation at the relentless teasing of his friend clear. But beneath that was something else. Something deeper.

But she couldn't yet tell what it was. She didn't know him well enough to read what he fought to conceal. Guilt? Heartbreak? Anger?

"Go away, *Your Grace*," he ground out.

Robert laughed as he tipped his head to her in mock salute and then glided into the crowd and left them alone.

"I'm sorry about him," Tyndale murmured. "He's…well, he's Roseford. He means no harm."

"Is he really trying to uncover my true identity?" she asked, wishing her voice didn't tremble so.

He turned his face and sighed. She could tell the answer already. "I wasn't certain you would return. And I wanted to know why you ran away when you recognized me."

She caught her breath. "*You* asked him to find out who I was?"

"Robert has avenues to investigate that I do not," he said. "So yes, I did ask him to try."

"Does he know? Do *you* know?" Her heart throbbed at the idea and the questions about what he would do now if he did realize who she was. What relationship she had to the woman he had been prepared to marry.

His forehead wrinkled. "Why are you so afraid? Why were you so afraid the last time we were together? How do you know me? Or more importantly, how do I know you?"

She moved to turn away, but he caught her arm. Her skin practically hissed as his fingers closed over her bare flesh. She slowly lifted her gaze to his and found him focused very intently on her mouth, despite the adversarial bent of the conversation between them. She licked her lips and felt the shudder move through him in response.

There was something powerful about it, the fact that she could move him physically, even if his pursuit was still abjectly terrifying.

"Wh-why would you think I knew you?" she asked, trying to keep her tone light.

"Don't lie," he whispered. "When you saw me without my mask, your reaction was immediate and powerful. Visceral. You ran away without so much as a look back. I know you know who I am."

"I—" she began, but could say no more.

He leaned in closer. His breath stirred her skin and she wanted so desperately to lean into it, into *him*, once more. Her mind was spinning and her body singing for her to melt against him. Surrender herself in every way she could think of.

"Say it," he demanded.

"Please don't—"

"Say it. Say who I am," he repeated, his gray eyes growing more intense than ever.

"Tyndale," she heard her voice say. "The Duke of Tyndale. *Matthew.*"

He shifted when she said the last, his Christian name, and his gaze fluttered once more over her body. Like hearing it woke some side of him that wasn't proper.

"That's right," he said, his voice suddenly rougher, lower. "You *do* know me. But if you ran, it has to be because you thought I might know you. Are you…" He trailed off and seemed to gather himself. "Are you the wife of a friend?"

She jerked her arm from his, the spell between them not quite broken, but lessened in the face of his suggestion. "What are you accusing me of?"

"Plenty of unhappy ladies come to this place seeking the kind of anonymous pleasure you did," he said. "But if your husband is a friend of mine, that would change that night between us. Turn it into—"

"No!" she interrupted. "I told you the last time we were together, I am a widow. And I was not married to anyone you would know. At least not anyone you would likely recognize even if you'd seen him a dozen times."

He tilted his head. "The way you say that, it makes me think…was he a servant? Or someone I encountered in their trade?"

She stiffened. He was so certain that her reasons to run had to do with her late husband. There was no reason to disabuse him of that notion. Let him think that Gregory was the connection that had caused her to flee and he wouldn't go looking for her uncle.

"Yes," she lied. "*Yes*, you knew him. I'd seen you before, just in passing. Our worlds were never meant to cross as they did that night, Your Grace."

"Matthew," he corrected softly.

"I'm sorry?"

"If I am going to bury my tongue between your thighs, I think we're past the point of you calling me Your Grace."

She held his stare for a moment, shivering at the direct way he'd described their encounter. At the heat that laced his tone and his expression even now.

"*Are* you going to do that again?" she found herself asking. Bold, too bold.

"You ran before," he said, his fingers lifting to trace the skin of her cheek, dancing just along the edge of her mask. The edge of danger. "Why would you want to come back?"

She swallowed, and this time she didn't have to lie to him. "I was…*shocked* when I recognized you without the mask. Terrified at what would happen next. So I did run. But I couldn't stop…thinking about what happened between us that night, Your Grace." He shot her a look. "Matthew," she whispered, loving the feel of his name on her tongue. "*That's* why I came back. But I-I don't want you to know who I am."

His fingers fell away. "You would have me exposed and still protect yourself."

She hesitated a fraction. "If you knew why, you'd understand my need to do this. It isn't fair, I suppose, and if you want to walk away, find a connection that is less complicated, I understand."

She held her breath as she awaited his answer. She told herself it was about the investigation she had come here to pursue. But it wasn't. She wanted him to agree to continue with her for far more than that. It was desire that drove her as much as truth. Need as much as justice.

He had somehow inspired that in her.

"I didn't think you'd come back," he said softly, and shifted closer to her. Close enough that she could just lift her hand and press it against that strong chest. When she did so, he hissed out a sound of pleasure. "I *wanted* you to come back."

He was leaning in now, his mouth moving toward hers. "You did?" she managed to squeak out. "Why?"

He didn't answer with words, but brushed his mouth over hers. All thought, all question, all fear dissipated with that touch. She fisted her hand against his chest as his arms came around her, drew her in closer while he deepened the kiss. She was lost. Found.

And in that moment she didn't give a damn about investigating anything more than whatever this spark was between them. The rest could wait.

Matthew entered the chamber that had been assigned to him and his stranger, and let out a ragged sigh. He felt on edge with desire. Wild with it, and that was not something he'd truly ever experienced before. It swelled inside him, loud and powerful. It took over any guilt he felt. It swallowed all his hesitation. It spoke to him in a guttural language that was as old and powerful as time itself.

And what it said was to take this woman. Claim her. Mark her as his.

He shuddered and pushed that thought aside, along with all the others.

"Come here," he whispered as he moved toward the bed.

She followed his directive silently, but her hand trembled as she reached for him. He smiled. So he moved her as much as she moved him. Despite whatever kept her in that mask, her desire was real.

He wanted to bathe in it. Let it wash him clean and set him free like it had the last time he touched her. She looked up at him, and he caught his breath as he drank in the sight of her. She was truly exquisite. Her features were delicate, at least those he could see. Her dark eyes sparkled as she let them flit over him nervously. They matched her silky hair to perfection and he lifted a hand to gently smooth it over the loose chignon. Little tendrils cascaded from the style, created pathways over her exposed collarbone and the column of her throat.

He leaned in to trace one of those pathways with his lips. She made a soft groan and her hands came up to tangle in his hair. His mask bumped her neck, and he lifted his head with a frown.

"Since you know who I am," he said, and reached up to untie the mask. "I think I can remove this."

She caught her breath as he did so and tracked his movements as he set the mask away on the bedside table. When he returned his lips to her neck, she sighed again and he devoted himself to nibbling and sucking his way along the elegant column. She tasted like…honey, like spiced wine. Sweet and intoxicating. A flavor he wanted to lose himself in.

And he would. For a while. His hands slid around her back and as he continued to kiss her, he found the line of buttons along her gown. He unfastened each one slowly, letting his fingers stroke the shockingly bare skin beneath.

"Why no undergarments?" he murmured against her throat.

She shifted. "I-it felt m-more outrageous," she stammered, her voice strained as he sucked her neck gently. "Oh…"

He lifted his head and met her unsteady gaze. "You liked the danger of coming here," he said softly. "The uncertainty."

She nodded slowly. "My life has always been…arranged. My future will be, too, soon enough. Coming here was a rebellion. A claiming of what I want, if only for a little while."

He stared at her. This was supposed to be a moment stolen from time, wrapped in anonymity. Except she knew who he was now. And she was confessing secrets that were powerful.

Secrets that inspired him to go wild, to forget that he was a rational man of control. With her, he wanted to be more.

"What *do* you want, Miss *Swan*?" he asked, using that

secret name Robert had uncovered in his investigation into her
identity.

Her throat fluttered at the question and she stared up at him,
her lips trembling, her breath coming short so that it lifted her
utterly delectable breasts on each inhalation.

"I want you," she whispered, dark color filling her cheeks
with every pointed word. "What happened between us, it was
never like that with my husband. It was never like that with
just...just my...my hand."

He shifted as his mind moved to images of this woman
spread out before him, touching herself for his pleasure. For her
own. He shook the thoughts off.

"How do you want me?" he whispered as he hooked his
fingers into the neckline of her gown and gently tugged it
forward, baring her from the waist up.

She swallowed. "Hard," she gasped. "Fast. With your
mouth, with your fingers, with your cock. I don't care. I just
want you. I don't know enough to ask for anything more."

"Then let me show you," he growled, shocked by his own
words. He sounded like Robert at his swaggering, drawling,
seductive best...or worst. But that had never been Matthew. And
yet here he was, inspired to tug this stranger's gown the rest of
the way off. Inspired to tug her naked body flush against his as
he drove his tongue deep within her mouth and showed her that
he wanted her.

As he imagined every wicked, wild thing his mind had ever
conjured and planned how to fulfill those fantasies until she was
shaking in release beneath him.

He caught her hips and lifted her, cupping her bottom as he
ground her down over his aching cock. She dipped her head back
on a gasp and her legs came around his hips to hold herself
steady. He smiled as he moved them across the room like this
and pressed her hard against the wall. She lifted against him, soft
sounds lost on his tongue as he fumbled with the placard on his
trousers. Finally he managed to get the buttons loose and he
popped free, his cock brushing her backside. He hissed at the

touch of heat on heat, hardness against soft.

He wanted her. To be inside of her. And his mind kept screaming *now*. *Now*. *Now*! Everything else was lost. All his usual control was gone, and he reached between them to press his fingers against her sex. She was wet, hot to the touch, and he shuddered as he moved himself in place and drove hard into her waiting body.

She cried out at the breach and ground against him, likely out of pure instinct. But the cry broke their mouths, and as she looked at him, their faces so close together, the intensity of that connection only drove the power of the other. He held her stare as he drove her against the wall, pivoting his hips just so, withdrawing as far as he could before he took again and again.

He watched her as she met his rhythm. Watched the wonder in her expression transform to wanton desire and deepen to the edge of release. And then he watched her plummet off that edge. Her body milked him as she dug her nails into his shirt and rode out the pleasure. Only when she went limp in his arms did he carry her back to the bed and part their bodies to lay her across the pillows.

She stared up at him, dark eyes glazed as they slid down his body and settled on his still hard and now very wet cock. "You didn't—" she said.

He shook his head. "Not yet. I'm savoring this. You wouldn't dare deny me that, would you?"

She sat up and caught his cravat, with a tug, she pulled him in close. "I think it's evident I wouldn't dare deny you anything."

She kissed him. Slowly. And he let her trace her tongue over his lips. Let her come inside and gently, carefully explore as he had explored. She flattened her hand on his chest and pushed him back until he lay across the bed with her leaning over him. Only then did she part their mouths and begin to untie his cravat, unfasten his shirt. He placed his arms beneath his head and smiled up at her.

"Seduction looks well on you, Miss Swan."

She blushed. "It sounds so silly for you to call me that."

She opened his shirt and swallowed hard. He almost puffed with a pride that felt so very odd. He was not one to preen and here he did so as she lifted a trembling hand and laid it to his flesh.

"You want to tell me your real name?" he asked, trying to focus on the conversation rather than the fact that she was smoothing that soft, delicate hand down his stomach, to the waist of his open trousers, closer and closer to the cock that still throbbed and demanded attention.

If he weren't careful, he'd be unmanned the moment she touched him. And that wasn't what he had in mind for the rest of this night.

"No," she said, darting her gaze from his face and settling it on the same cock he'd been pondering. "That would be a very bad idea."

He frowned, but didn't press. Anonymity, it seemed, would reign, at least for her. And then she touched him and he no longer cared about that or anything else.

She took his length in her hand and smoothed her fingers from tip to base. He lifted up into her with a grunt, and she smiled. A wicked little smile on an otherwise very sweet and ladylike face. At least the part he could see.

"I have watched those around me in this place," she said. "With much interest."

He arched a brow as she stroked him again and electric sensation raced through his entire body. "Did you now?"

"I saw more than I ever imagined, but I was always interested in one particular act."

He sat up on his elbows and watched as she inched a little lower. "What act is that?"

She positioned herself so those full, luscious lips were just beside his cock. His heart had begun to throb. "This one," she whispered, then darted her tongue out and swirled it around the tip of him. She glanced up and met his eyes. Hers were wide. "I taste myself on you."

He grunted. "You will kill me, I think."

She smiled again and then lowered her mouth over him a second time. This time, though, she was not teasing. Whatever she'd watched in the masquerade, whatever she knew or didn't know but had observed…she was a good student of the wanton arts. She took him into her mouth as deep as she could and stroked him in time with her hand.

Pleasure jolted through him with every motion, and he dipped his head back with a long, unsteady moan. It had been ages since he had this experience, and he'd forgotten just how good a woman's tongue felt as it swirled around his cock, what kind of desire the pressure of it could create. How it made a man want to surrender whatever small power he had and worship any woman who gave such unselfish pleasure.

She built him toward completion like it was a race, and he had no control left to fight her. His mind was emptying, his hips lifting, he just kept growling out incoherent sounds of need as his balls tightened and the pleasure reached its peak.

When it did, he grunted and pulled free just as he came. She didn't recoil, but continue to pump him with her hand until he gasped out surrender and collapsed into a boneless, tingling heap.

Only then did she cuddle into his side and wrap her arm around him as they lay together in satisfied silence. And for just a moment, it felt perfect.

CHAPTER EIGHT

Isabel didn't know how long they lay together in the silence of that warm room. It felt like a blissful eternity as his hands traced her naked hip and hers made trails along his chest and stomach. At last, she looked up into his face. His eyes were closed and she drank in the sight.

He was relaxed and that gave his expression a warmer look, rather than the tense one he normally had. His short-cropped beard shadowed a well-defined jaw and highlighted equally sharp cheekbones. He was truly a beautiful man. Like he had stepped from a painting.

There was no doubt why Angelica had loved him.

That thought pierced the warm fog Isabel had allowed herself to surrender to, and she tensed a little as she withdrew back into reality. Pleasure was wonderful, but she had a duty to perform here, as well.

"May I ask you a question?" Her voice cracked and she swallowed hard.

He didn't open his eyes, but his full lips quirked up a little. "The perfect time to interrogate a man is after an experience like that. I'd give you the keys to the kingdom if I had them."

"Why did your friend say that you were being brought back from the dead?"

He went stiff beside her, and slowly his gray eyes opened. The tension was back on his face immediately, and she marked how that put a distance between them. One she surprisingly did not like, despite her reasons for being here.

She preferred the sensual man without a care to the one who suddenly looked...broken.

"What happened to a stolen night?" he asked, his tone suddenly neutral, purposefully unreadable. "Anonymity?"

"But you are not anonymous," she responded. "Your Grace."

He sat up and pushed from the bed and her arms. He pulled his shirt closed and began to button it before he tucked it into his trousers and fastened them, too.

"No, I suppose I am not," he said at last as he turned away from her. She watched his every movement and did her best not to react. "And since that is true, I'm surprised you ask the question."

"Why?"

He faced her, his eyebrow arched and his lips thin with displeasure. "Everyone knows my story, don't they? It is all they talk about. *The Duke of Tyndale and His Tragedy*. It is practically folklore."

She sucked in a breath at his brittle tone. But was it mournful or angry? She couldn't tell. He hid that too well.

"I admit, I know a...little about what happened," she said carefully as she thought of the cousin she had known and played with all those years ago. She tried to picture Angelica with this man and felt a stab of powerful jealousy that she shoved aside.

He shook his head. "I'm sure you do. Which is why I'm confused as to why you'd ask about Roseford's comment. If I am being brought back from the dead, it is because part of me was buried with my fiancée." He turned away. "Or so the story goes."

"So the story goes," she repeated, and stood up. She wrapped herself in the sheet and moved toward him. "Does that mean it is untrue?"

He continued to stare out the window in the chamber, his expression blank. "Sometimes it feels like more than a part of me died with her. And yet I am still here. And I get to live with the consequences of what I did."

She gripped a fist at her side. What he did? That sounded like a confession. One that might prove her uncle right in all his accusations when he railed out his hate and his rage toward this man. Her stomach turned at the idea that Tyndale...Matthew...could truly be a killer.

"What did you do?" she whispered.

He straightened up and slowly faced her. "It is not a topic I wish to discuss with a stranger," he said softly. "But it is what Robert referred to when he said what he said. I suppose that by coming here, by being with you...I'm getting better in his eyes."

"And in your own?" she asked, meeting those very eyes now. Trying desperately to see if he was victim or villain in them. Unable to determine anything but that they were dilated with renewed desire as he let them flit over her. Unable to control her own reaction to that longing, despite the unsatisfying answers to her inquiries.

"I feel like I'm alive again when you touch me," he whispered. "And I want that. Just as I want you."

He took the hand that held the sheet and tugged it free so that the cover fell away and left her naked. "I suppose we must test how long they allow us to keep this room occupied."

She smiled and set aside her questions. She just needed to get closer to obtain more information. And closer was exactly what she wanted right now.

"I do have one request," she said as he moved in and pressed his lips to the curve of her collarbone.

"What's that?" he asked, his tone muffled as he kissed her skin.

"This time I need you naked," she said, shocked by how wanton her words were. Her tone.

"I would never deny a lady," he said as he tugged her back toward the bed. "Not now, not ever."

Isabel's hands shook as she rode the last few miles to her uncle's home. It was late, well after three, and her body ached with all the pleasures she had explored with Matthew that night. As a lover, he was gentle but passionate, demanding but giving. He tended to her pleasure over and over, and when he took his?

Well, his loss of control was a sight to behold. One that made her sex throb once more with need.

How she wished she could just focus on those wanton memories. The very ones she'd been wanting to create when she started going to the Donville Masquerade. The ones that were supposed to keep her warm and satisfied when she was forced to share a cold and perfunctory bed with whatever merchant or lower gentleman her uncle eventually matched her with.

Only the other topic of their night together kept interrupting her pleasant memories. And that topic was Angelica.

Her heart lurched at the reminder that her cousin had once owned this man's heart. Certainly, she must have also enjoyed his body, as well. How could anyone have him and not want to touch him?

And yet Angelica was dead and Matthew's answers hadn't fully satisfied Isabel's questions on the matter. When he spoke of her, it was with sharpness. But was that because he felt the unfairness of losing her so young? Or frustration that her death was always linked to him, so he could never leave those memories that haunted him behind?

Or was it what her uncle suspected? That a mention of Angelica set Matthew off because of a guilty conscience? A murderer's hate?

That didn't seem right. It didn't settle in with truth in her heart.

She scrubbed a hand over her face. "Bollocks," she muttered softly since no one could hear her swear.

Angelica. How stunning she had been with that honey hair and those huge blue eyes. She'd been a rare beauty, and Isabel had always felt somewhat plain beside her. Angelica had been made for all her finery, and she wore it all with enviable confidence.

As girls, they'd been close. But as Angelica took her place in Society, as she came out to the attention of dukes and earls and viscounts, Isabel had been less and less involved. Visits had dwindled, letters had gone from once a week to once a month…once in a blue moon. Angelica had found her place and it hadn't included Isabel, who was by then married to Gregory and settling in to the life of the bride of a solicitor.

A very empty life that had been, while Angelica had captured the attention of…*him*. Matthew. Now Isabel's heart pounded and she cursed herself for it. For what she knew she felt, what she'd been feeling over and over.

Jealousy. Strong and ugly.

The hack came to a stop around the back of her uncle's home, and she paid the driver before she took a deep breath and looked up at the house. This was not her home. She didn't remember the last place she'd truly felt was her home. With her parents, perhaps, years ago. A lifetime.

She sighed and snuck up the back path to the servants' entrance that she paid a footman to keep unlocked when she took these little adventures. She slipped into the kitchen and locked the door behind her, shaking off her night and the troubling thoughts and memories it inspired. She was here again, and she had to slip back into her normal life and not show that she was changed by Matthew's touch. By the questions about him that now haunted her.

By her own reactions to both.

She walked into the hall and toward the back stair that would return her to her bedchamber, but she had not yet turned into it when she heard the sound of a throat being cleared behind her. She froze and slowly turned to find her uncle standing at the entrance to his study, arms folded as he glared at her in silent accusation.

"Uncle Fenton," she said, her heart leaping to her throat and lodging there so words were nearly impossible to form. "I-I was…that is, I needed…I mean to say—"

"Don't choke on your lies, girl," he said, stepping aside to motion her into his study.

She bent her head and trudged toward him. She was caught, there was nothing else to it. Tonight of all nights, too.

"Sit," he said as he shut the door behind them.

She moved to the settee and perched there, watching as he moved to the sideboard where he poured himself scotch. To her surprise, he also poured a second tumbler, this one of sherry. He handed her the second and took a seat across from hers.

He sipped his drink before he said, "Where have you been?"

She swallowed hard. She'd never been a very good liar. It wasn't in her nature, despite the sneaking out and scandalous behavior she'd been allowing herself of late. Those activities had been born of desperation, not a point of character. Now she fought to find words that would save her.

Because the truth would most definitely not set her free in this case.

"I suppose my saying I was just in the kitchen getting myself a bite wouldn't be accepted?" she asked.

He shook his head. "It would not. You were out. I saw you return in a hack, of all things. Where were you?"

She folded her arms. "I was out...seeing Sarah," she lied. "Her mother is not well and I sometimes go out at night to help her."

He arched a brow as if he didn't quite believe that. "And you take a hack to do this, rather than simply requesting one of my carriages?"

She worried her lip. "I did not want to impose upon your hospitality more than I already have," she said. "Or trouble you and your servants."

He stared at her a long time, those eyes that were so like her cousin's boring into her. She shifted beneath the weight of that stare and the lies that caused it.

"Perhaps you just don't want me to know where you're going," he said softly. "Or what you're doing in truth."

Her mouth was so dry that it felt almost glued shut. She took a great gulp of her sherry before she whispered, "I assure you not, uncle."

He shrugged. "Lie if you'd like, but there is no point to it. You have lived here for how long?"

She pressed her lips together. "For a little over a year," she said. "A boundless hospitality that I feel very grateful for, I assure you."

"That's right." Her uncle suddenly sounded far away. "You moved into my home thirteen days after the second anniversary of her death."

Isabel flinched. There was Angelica again, always the other person in any room where she entered. The marker of before and after. "Yes," she whispered.

"And you are out of mourning for that husband your father arranged for you, yes?" Uncle Fenton continued. "The time has officially passed?"

"Er, yes," Isabel said. "It's been about eighteen months since his passing."

"Good." He got up and paced to the window. "Very good. I think it is time to put you back out on the marriage mart, Isabel."

She gulped for air. This was something he danced around, of course. The idea of matching her again had been the driving force that sent her to the Donville Masquerade in the first place. But tonight her uncle seemed more…driven by the idea. Like it was a plan, not just a fleeting notion.

"Oh, Uncle Fenton," she said. "That is very kind of you, of course, to think of my future. But I do not know if I am ready to—"

"Ready?" he repeated, as if he was confused. "What does ready have to do with it? You cannot stay here forever, my melancholy cannot be good for you. It is time to make a new arrangement. Better than the last, certainly. Your father should have come to me then. You could have had a knight or even a minor baron to wed. But he was insistent that my money and name not influence. Well, that is over now. We'll find you a true gentleman."

"You wish...you wish to take me out into the *ton*?"

He blinked. "Of course, where else would I match you? I know little of merchants and the like. It's time you find a match and that is what we'll do. Attach a little dowry to you and you'll be away from whatever trouble you're finding for yourself before this Season is over."

Her heart lurched. The very idea of coming out into Society, of being thrown back into the constriction and loneliness that a marriage could create...oh, her whole body hurt at the very idea of it.

"Please," she whispered. "Could I not just stay a widow? I have very little, I know, but I would not have to stay here. I could find some other arrangement, perhaps even take on a position in a household or—"

He wrinkled his nose. "A position? I will not have it said that I sent my niece to *trade*. You should be happy, Isabel. Soon you will have a husband, perhaps even one with a little title. Most young women would trip over themselves to take that future. Now, go up to bed. That's enough of this nonsense."

He waved her toward the door before he took a place back at his desk. He bent his head, took up a quill and began to write, signaling in no uncertain terms that the conversation was over.

Isabel shivered as she got to her feet and walked from the room. This night had begun and ended with uncertainty. Even the intense passion and pleasure in the middle couldn't change that fact.

Nor the fact that the control of her life had just been snatched from her hands. And now she was the mercy of a man deep in grieving and revenge. One who would explode if he ever discovered where she had truly been going.

And with whom she had been spending her nights.

CHAPTER NINE

Matthew sat in his cousin Ewan's parlor. He was quiet as his cousin, mute since birth, signed and his wife Charlotte translated their secret language. Alongside the couple were Ewan and Matthew's closest friend from childhood, Baldwin, and his wife of just a year, Helena. Normally Matthew relished these times with them, with all the dukes in their club. And seeing these particular dukes so happy was even better.

But his mind kept returning, time and time again, to his stranger at the Donville Masquerade. His swan. It had been two days since he saw her, touched her, and his nights had been restless with dreams of her. His days just as distracted by the same.

"Don't you think, Matthew?" Charlotte asked.

He jolted at his name and looked up to see the foursome all looking at him expectantly. Of course he had no idea to what that question referred.

"Er, I...I'm sorry, Charlotte. I admit I was leagues away," he said with an apologetic tilt of his head. "Forgive me."

Charlotte had always been kind and her gentle expression now grew worried, as did the faces of the others. They even exchanged looks, and his stomach tightened. Since Angelica's death, there had been a lot of those kinds of looks between his friends. God, how he hated their pity.

"Charlotte, you were telling me about the nursery," Helena said with a smile for Baldwin. "I'd love to see what you've done."

Charlotte smiled, but with her pregnancy so far along, she struggled to get up. Ewan moved toward her, helping her to her feet before he settled a hand on her stomach gently. He smiled, but there was tension to his face as she leaned in to kiss his cheek.

"Yes, you gentlemen will excuse us, won't you?" Charlotte asked.

They were all on their feet by then, and Matthew inclined his head as the two ladies departed, leaving him alone with his two best friends. It should have been so comfortable. Ewan had been raised by Matthew's father and mother. Because of his inability to speak, his own family had been abominable to him, and Matthew's late father hadn't stood for it. In the end, they had been raised as brothers, not just cousins or friends.

And Baldwin was nearly as close. His father had been good friends with Matthew's. The families had always been linked. Baldwin and his sister Charlotte had been a constant part of their lives. Ewan had even fallen in love with Charlotte when they were just children.

They were a bonded group within the larger group of their friends. And yet there was no ease in being alone with them, because they knew nothing about Matthew's recent troubles.

Baldwin sighed as he went to the parlor door and shut it. When he looked at them, he shook his head. "I don't know which of you two to start with. You're both like ghosts. Is there something horrible going on that I know nothing about?"

"Start with him," Matthew said, indicating Ewan.

Ewan glared at him but pulled out the small silver notebook he used to communicate. The engraved piece, given to him by his wife, reflected the firelight as he scribbled out a shaky message. "*It's the baby.*"

Matthew read the note out loud and his stomach dropped as he jerked his face back up to Ewan's. "Is something wrong?"

Ewan swallowed and wrote, "*Charlotte is healthy and the baby moves and kicks. I would be delighted. I am delighted.*

But..."

He stopped writing midsentence, set the notebook down and walked away. Both Matthew and Baldwin read the message, and Matthew exchanged a look with their friend.

"Ewan," he said softly, pushing his own troubles away to focus on Ewan. "Are you still worried this child will inherit your...affliction?"

Ewan didn't have to answer in writing. The way his neck stiffened, the way his knuckles whitened, was enough.

"It's why you pushed my sister away for so long," Baldwin said, his tone just as kind as Matthew's had been. "Why you nearly didn't marry her despite the feelings you have for one another."

Ewan jerked out a nod, and Matthew was shocked to see the tears sparkle in his cousin's eyes. He moved on him, catching his arm with both his hands. "You know we will all love, protect and spoil this baby no matter what. He or she will never know a lack of acceptance. A lack of family."

Ewan swallowed hard and patted Matthew's hand before he walked back to the notebook. "*I know. I still worry. Charlotte sees it. She comforts me, too. Sometimes, though, I can't help but fear for the future.*"

"You don't regret your decision to take this life with my sister, do you?" Baldwin asked, his tone suddenly sharper.

Ewan jolted and he scraped out in all capitals, "*NEVER!*" He drew a few long breaths as if to calm himself and then he wrote. "*The baby comes in a few weeks. Diana will be helping Charlotte with the birth. And then we'll see.*"

Matthew nodded. Diana was their friend Lucas's wife, and a talented healer. "Yes, we'll see. In the end, that is all any of us get, you know. Tragedy can strike in an instant to any of us. Don't go looking for it if you can avoid it."

"*Your mother said as much to me when I was still tangled up over a future with Charlotte.*" Ewan smiled.

Matthew returned the expression. "Well, she is, as you know, always correct."

"Is that why you're *so troubled? Angelica?"*

Baldwin arched a brow. "I've some thoughts on that subject."

"Thoughts," Matthew repeated. "Really?"

Baldwin shot Ewan a look. "I've heard he's been spending time at the Donville Masquerade with Robert."

Matthew's eyes went wide. "Who told you that?"

"Hugh said the three of you went there when you all snuck out of James and Emma's party. But that *you've* kept going back." Baldwin folded his arms. "Are you denying it?"

"No," Matthew said. "Why should I?"

To his surprise, Ewan slapped his arm hard. *"Good. It's time to come back to your life, Matthew. We've all longed to see you do so."*

"So is it *guilt* that makes you look so ragged?" Baldwin asked.

Matthew sighed. In truth, he wasn't opposed to talking to the two of them about his troubles. Though both would be shocked, they cared for him and would not judge. And he needed an opinion on the matter that wasn't from Robert and his skewed view on life and passion.

"There is a...lady," he said.

Both men drew back, and their shock was clear. "A lady?" Baldwin repeated.

"A woman," Matthew corrected. "She sometimes seems like a lady, though she implied she might be a servant or that she comes from trade. I met her that first night I went with Hugh and Robert. I've gone back because of her."

Ewan drew a long breath and began to write. *"Not that I've had much experience with such things, but even I've heard of the Donville Masquerade. Is it as wicked as described?"*

Matthew pursed his lips as images of naked bodies, roaming hands, arching backs filled his mind. Images of his swan, writhing above him as she cried out her pleasure. It put his body on edge as he ground out, "Yes."

"Does that mean she's your lover?"

Matthew shifted at the question in black and white before him. He'd never been one to brag about his conquests, not that he'd had any in what felt like a lifetime.

"Yes."

"Good God," Baldwin breathed. "That is not what I expected. I thought you were just leaning on the wall, cursing Robert for his interference."

"It started that way," Matthew said, running a hand through his hair to expel some of the restless energy this topic created low in his belly. "He dragged me there, and you know how hard it is to resist him. But I didn't intend for *this*."

"*How did it start?*" Ewan wrote.

Matthew shut his eyes. He could picture that first night so perfectly. "She was being harassed," he said. "I couldn't let that stand. I stepped in, we talked, I was shocked by this instant connection."

Baldwin smiled softly. "I know a bit about that."

Matthew shook his head, for he didn't think he ought to compare the connection he felt to his lover to Baldwin's deep and abiding love for Helena.

"We ended up on the terrace," he continued.

"I also know a bit about that," Baldwin said, laughing this time.

"Well, it snowballed," Matthew said. "We kissed. And the next time I saw her, it was more than kissing. We are lovers, despite all my reservations and questions. I can't stop thinking about her. Dreaming about her."

"That is a good thing, isn't it?" Baldwin asked. "A natural thing for a man to want a woman. Why do you hesitate?"

"First, she wears a mask," Matthew explained. "I don't know her identity."

Ewan's eyes were wide but he wrote nothing, just stared. Baldwin even looked shocked. "Well, that is something," he said slowly. "It is a masquerade, though. You must do the same."

"I did," Matthew said. "But she knows my identity. It's a long story. I do hesitate that she knows me but I know nothing about her."

"*That's fair,*" Ewan wrote. "*It's also not your only hesitation.*"

Matthew pursed his lips. "You know me too well. I forget that sometimes until you so rudely remind me. No, that's not all." He paced the room. "Being with this woman, despite the hidden identities and the wild start to it…it feels like coming back to life. But it also feels like betrayal."

Baldwin flinched. "Angelica has been gone for a long time, Tyndale," he said gently.

"You think I should just pack up any feelings about her and move on?" Matthew snapped.

Baldwin shook his head. "Of course not. No one expects the pain of losing her to go away completely. I could not imagine the grief of what you've endured, I know that even more strongly since Helena came into my life. But I also can't picture that Angelica would have wanted you to go on in misery, holding up her memory for the rest of your days."

Matthew walked to the sideboard. He fiddled with the bottles without pouring himself a drink. He didn't want one—he just didn't want to look at the two men who knew him best. Not when they might see what he, himself, didn't want to explore too deeply.

"I know you are right," he said softly.

He could say no more. They didn't push for more, they just let the silence hang between them for a moment. Then Baldwin came to stand beside him and slung an arm around his shoulders.

"Did you get the invitation to Lord and Lady Callis's ball on Saturday night?"

Matthew wrinkled his brow. "Yes, I think so. Mother mentioned it, as well, when I called on her a few days ago. What about it?"

"Well, all of us are going. You know he married his mistress last year and the duchesses seem determined to help make her entry into Society easier."

Matthew bent his head at the kindness of his friends and

their beautiful wives. "That sounds like the duchesses."

"Why don't you come? Get out into Society, shake off the melancholy and confusion with your friends. Make your mother happy."

Matthew glanced over to find Ewan nodding his agreement. He sighed. "Very well. I've been spending too much time brooding in hells as it is. A night with friends would probably do me some good."

Baldwin grinned. "I think it will be just the thing. You take a night away from this woman, clear your head. Perhaps it will help you see things more clearly."

Matthew nodded, and at that moment Helena and Charlotte returned to the room together. He watched as his friends greeted their wives, the light that returned to both men obvious.

They were right, of course, that a night away from the hell, away from his search for his stranger, would likely do him good. But the idea that it could clear his head seemed foolish, indeed. Because his mind was tangled and there didn't seem to be a way to unravel it. Not yet. Perhaps not ever.

CHAPTER TEN

Isabel shifted and slid her hands along her skirt nervously. The ball spun around her, a familiar dizzy mix of loud music, chattering voices and twirling skirts. In theory, it was very much like a dozen other balls she had attended over the years.

In truth, it felt different—because this was a ball thrown by a viscount and his wife. The room was filled with earls and dukes, second sons and those who had inherited all they had and more.

She felt very out of place.

"What did you think of Callis?" her uncle asked as he handed over a drink.

She sipped it gingerly before she said, "The viscount and his wife were very friendly."

That was true, at least. The viscount was a handsome man and his wife was beautiful and sweet. They were clearly in love, something that surprised Isabel, for she knew many Society marriages were arranged and loveless.

Not that she could talk.

Uncle Fenton hurrumphed. "*She* didn't used to be so high and mighty," he said.

Isabel let her gaze slip to the viscountess again. "No?"

"It's unseemly to talk about," her uncle said with a shake of his head. "I should not have brought it up. But since there is a bit of scandal to the couple, I thought it wouldn't be a bad start for you in Society."

Isabel pressed her lips together hard at the veiled insult. "Thank you, uncle."

He shrugged. "I don't mean because of any scandal associated with you," he explained. "Unless there is more to your sneaking out than I yet know. But because everyone is judging her, perhaps you would feel their judgment less."

Isabel sighed. She supposed, in his own way, he was being kind. Trying to make it easier. It wasn't though.

They stood together in silence for a moment as she stared out over the crowd. She felt so on the outside of this world. Pressed against the glass but unable to truly enter. She had rather hoped Sarah might come tonight, but her mother's illness had prevented it.

So Isabel was truly alone even in the crowded room.

"Isabel!"

She turned at Uncle Fenton's call and found that he was no longer alone. A gentleman stood next to him. He was tall, broad-shouldered, not unhandsome. But he was likely a contemporary of her uncle, older than Isabel by at least twenty-five years.

Her heart sank.

"May I present Mrs. Isabel Hayes," her uncle said. "Isabel, this is Sir Daniel Goodacre."

"Sir Daniel," she said, extending her hand.

He caught it and lifted it to his lips. As he brushed them over her gloved knuckles, she tried to keep her smile on her face. He was staring at her breasts. Of course he was.

"Mrs. Hayes," he drawled. "You are a vision."

Uncle Fenton smiled at the man. "Sir Daniel is an old friend," he said.

"It is a pleasure to meet you," Isabel said as she extracted her hand from his grip.

She fought the urge to shake it out. Shake off his touch. God's teeth, she was traveling down the same road her father had put her on. Her uncle might marry her higher, but it was practically to the same man.

"I wondered if your dance card was full this evening, Mrs.

Hayes," Sir Daniel asked with a side glance for her uncle.

She swallowed. "Indeed, it is not, for we only just arrived."

"Then might I be so bold as to ask you to dance the next with me?" he said, motioning to the dancefloor where couples were just departing after the lilting end of the previous song.

Isabel inclined her head. This was the worst part of these events. While a woman might be asked to dance, it was only in theory that the answer could be no. In truth, she had more power at the Donville Masquerade than here in a public and presentable forum.

"Certainly," she said through clenched teeth. "It would be an honor."

He extended an arm and she took it. When she glanced back, she found a satisfied smile on her uncle's face. He almost looked as though everything had been determined. Her future taken care of so he could go back to ruthlessly grieving the past.

And her heart sank as the tones of a country jig began and she was forced to dance lightly while her entire being felt so desperately heavy.

Matthew stood along the wall as the ball went on around him, but he was not truly attending to it. His mind was turning to another room, another dancefloor, one that would shock the people in this room if they encountered it.

He was thinking of his stranger. His swan.

"Matthew!"

He turned and shook away those wicked thoughts as he watched his mother approach him. The duchess looked lovely in her finery, but he saw concern flash across her face before she leaned up to kiss his cheek.

"Mama," he said as he took her hand tucked it into the crook of his arm. "I'm so glad to find you. Would you like to take a turn on the dancefloor?"

She laughed as if the idea were absurd. "I will leave you to all the eligible ladies, I think. You know I do not dance."

"You should," he said, giving her a side glance. "You were always very good at it."

"With your father as partner," she said with a sad smile. "I doubt I'd be much good with someone else."

"Says the woman who is determined I find myself a new dance partner," he said as they looked out over the crowd together.

She squeezed his arm gently. "I push too hard, do I?"

He looked down at her, at that kind face he so adored. The one that had seen him through such grief. The one that wanted a future for him that he feared he could not provide.

"Not at all," he said softly. "You have my best interest at heart. How could I complain about that?"

"You can't," she said. "But you can certainly complain about my methods."

"I would not dare to do so," he teased. "And risk your wrath?"

His mother rolled her eyes. "My wrath that is of legend?"

He chuckled and felt a wave of comfort wash over him. He did feel more himself when he was with family and friends. The self he had settled into since Angelica's death. There was an ease to that, one he lost the moment he stepped into the masquerade and was confronted by burning desire that lit in him when he saw his stranger.

"You are very far away tonight," the duchess said. "Are you bored at the ball?"

He shrugged. "It is a ball. I suppose it's as fine a way to spend time as any other."

"Enthusiastic," she drawled. "So there is no one here who catches your interest?"

Matthew sighed as he let his gaze scan the room. He found friends aplenty, for most of the dukes had come to the party and were either gathered in clusters, talking to the other guests, or spinning around the floor with their brides. There were other friends to be found, as well. Friends outside his tight knit group, including their host.

But that wasn't what his mother meant about interest. She meant ladies. Unattached, marriageable ladies. Ones that would help eventually carry on his father's legacy by marrying him and birthing his sons.

"I don't—" he began, and then came to a stop. The crowd had parted slightly and revealed not a lady who caught his eye, but someone else. Someone far worse.

"What is it?" the duchess asked as she lifted on her tiptoes to gaze over the crowd with him.

"Fenton Winter," he breathed.

The name caused a visceral reaction in his mother. She caught her breath and grabbed for his arm with both hands. "Matthew," she whispered.

There was a reason for the strength of that reaction. Winter was Angelica's father. For years their families had gotten along. The man had approved of their match. But when she died, Winter had been truly devastated. He had rained down rage and heartbreak, as well as accusations, on Matthew's head.

Normally they did not attend the same events. Matthew made certain of that. But tonight there the man was. Over the years, he'd grown thinner. Gaunt, even. His jaw was set as he looked at the dancefloor, a line of displeasure that Matthew had come to know very well.

But he clearly had not yet seen Matthew, for he had no doubt Winter would have already come smashing across the ballroom for a public confrontation if he had.

"Perhaps I should go," he murmured.

His mother said something in reply, but he didn't hear her. In that moment, a lady came off the dancefloor and stopped in front of Winter. She had her back to Matthew—he could not see her face, but he didn't need to.

There was familiarity in the way she moved. The way her gown hung on her slender shoulders. In the dark, silky magic of her perfectly arranged hair.

That was…it looked like his swan. His stranger. His lover. And she was talking to Fenton Winter in a ballroom of a viscount, standing not fifty feet from Matthew.

"Matthew!" His mother's tone was sharp and pierced his stunned fog.

"Yes?" he asked, making himself look at her.

"What is wrong?" she asked. "Aside from Winter's being here, I mean. I've said your name three times."

He shook his head. "I'm sorry, I'm sorry, Mama. I don't know." He glanced back at Winter and his companion. She was still not facing him and his head began to spin. "I'm sorry. Excuse me."

He walked away from his mother, faintly aware of her saying his name yet again. He ignored it, too caught up in the swirling drumbeat of horror that was the situation unfolding before him. One he didn't understand completely, but recognized was not going to end well. How could it?

He staggered up to James and Emma, who were standing beside the dancefloor, heads close together, whispering and giggling to each other. When he interrupted them, James's expression immediately fell.

"What is it?" he asked, catching Matthew's arm.

Matthew felt glad for the grip. It brought him back to reality a bit. "I—Winter," he muttered.

James jerked his gaze in the direction Matthew looked and his eyes widened. "Christ, I'm sorry. I had no idea he would be here."

"Neither did I," Matthew gasped out. "Who is that woman with him?"

James looked again, as did Matthew. When they did, the lady finally pivoted to stand beside Winter, and Matthew got his first look at her face. And there was no longer any doubt or hope that she wasn't his stranger. He could tell by the shape of her lips, the curve of her jaw, the color of her dark eyes.

It was her.

James began to shake his head when Emma drew in a long

breath. "That is Isabel Hayes," she said gently. "She is...she's Angelica's cousin, Winter's niece. She has been staying with him for about a year. She's been in mourning most of that time, for her late husband."

Matthew's ears began to ring as he stared at the lady, the swan...*Isabel*, once more. She was even more beautiful when her face wasn't half covered by a mask.

"No." He choked on the word. "No."

"Matthew," James said. "Matthew, what is it?"

Matthew couldn't answer. He stared, unblinking, as Winter said something to Isabel and then stepped away from her into the milling crowd. She shifted, a look of discomfort crossing her face. Her lying, deceiving, utterly gorgeous face.

He said nothing to explain himself but headed off across the room toward her. The room was crowded, but it didn't matter. All he saw was her. All he could think about was her. Her and her lies and whatever horrible plan she had hatched in her head.

As he pushed through the groups of revelers, she turned, and her gaze settled on him. He watched emotion flood over her. Her eyes widened almost impossibly, her cheeks went bloodless, and in her gaze he saw abject terror.

All of which only proved what he knew all the more. She was his lady. And she had absolutely known exactly who and what he was.

He crossed the last few steps toward her and she pivoted, turning as if she would run. He didn't allow it. He caught her bare elbow and tugged her back, trying desperately to ignore the flash of heat and desire that rushed through him when his skin met hers.

"Come with me," he growled beneath his breath. "*Mrs. Hayes.*"

Isabel couldn't breathe as she was dragged through the

winding halls of Lord Callis's enormous house. Her vision was blurred and she couldn't hear over the pounding of her heart. She staggered, but Matthew didn't slow his pace, he just steadied her as he pushed into a parlor. As he released her, she staggered forward, flinching as he slammed the door behind them.

She didn't want to look at him and so she stood, eyes squeezed shut, hands fisted at her sides, her back to him. That moment stretched into an eternity before he barked out, "Turn around."

She was shaking from head to toe and tears stung her eyes as she slowly did as he ordered. He was still standing at the door, staring at her with his arms folded across that broad chest.

Gone was the lover who had so thoroughly tended to her needs over and over again. Gone was the man who confessed he was just as confused by the physical connection between them as she had been. Gone was all the softness and gentleness that made her believe he wasn't capable of hurting her cousin.

Left in the wake was rage, bubbling just below the surface. And contempt that turned his gorgeous gray eyes into stormy seas.

"Was it all a trap?" he snapped, his voice clipped. "A plot?"

She caught her breath at the accusation. At the emotion that echoed behind it. For a wild moment, she thought of lying, of denying she knew anything about what he asked. Of pretending she'd never been his stranger, his swan.

Only she couldn't. He arched a brow and it was clear that lie wouldn't save her any more than all the others had. The time had come for truth, and to let go of the brief foolishness that had placed her into his arms.

"No," she gasped, her voice sounding so rough and foreign. "I didn't know, not at first. I swear to you."

He laughed, but it was an ugly sound. "You swear, *Isabel*? *Mrs. Hayes*. Is that supposed to have meaning to me?"

She dropped her head. She deserved his censure, she knew. It still stung far more than it should have considering the fact she barely knew him. Couldn't have him. Despite the fact that everything between them was now over.

"I didn't know when I first met you," she repeated.

"But you did after," he growled, and paced past her farther into the room. "When? Was it before my mask came off? Was it before you bedded me?"

The hardness of the accusation slashed at her, and she struggled to maintain composure as she watched him walk to the fire. He pivoted and faced her, all darkness and anger now. And yet still utterly irresistible.

"No," she said. "Not before. It truly was when you were dressing after that…after that first time we were together and your mask came off that I knew. You remember my reaction, how I ran away. If I were already aware, why would I have done such a thing?"

For a fraction of a moment, the anger on his face faded. He nodded slowly. "I suppose that is a fair point."

She stepped toward him, her cheeks heating when he flinched. "Yes," she said. "I was horrified when I saw your face. Of all the men in the world that I could have just…just…"

"Fucked," he filled in.

She recoiled from that harsh word, one a lady was not meant to hear. Perhaps that was why he used it, to tell her he did not consider her a lady anymore. And why should he?

"Y-yes," she said, her voice shaking. "You were my cousin's—"

She stopped, for she couldn't say it. There was too much power to it.

He didn't seem to have those same reservations. "Your cousin's fiancé?" he asked, sneered. "Her killer."

She sucked in a breath at those words. "What?"

He moved forward now and she clenched her fists so that she would remain in place. "That is what your uncle thinks, isn't it? What he's fed to you over the years? Don't think I'm such a fool that I don't guess *that* is the reason you came back, sought me out, after you knew my name."

She bent her head. "I-I cannot deny it. I did come back, seek you out again, in part to…to…"

"Say it, Isabel," he growled. "Don't stop now."

"To investigate you," she finished on a sob.

His face twisted in disgust at that word. "You whored yourself to me in order to find out if I killed Angelica. On your uncle's orders?"

"No!" she said. "He doesn't know. He could never, *ever* know what I did."

His eyes narrowed, filled with disbelief. She'd earned that, of course. Earned all of his ill regard of her. His hate. But she didn't want it. Being this close to him, that wasn't what she wanted at all from the man who had awoken the desires she'd hidden. The man who had given her such pleasure.

"So you did it for your own interest," he said slowly. "And did you come to a decision about my guilt or innocence?"

"We did not meet often." Her voice shook and she couldn't control it. "But I could not believe that a man who—who—"

"Pleasured you," he said, his voice still hard even as his gaze flitted over her.

She nodded, her cheeks aflame once more at his bluntness. "Yes. But did it so…sweetly. With such attentiveness and care when he did not have to give either…I couldn't believe a man whose first act was to protect me could have hurt Angelica."

His jaw set, rippled. She wished she could touch that hard cheek, trace it with her fingers as she had once done and now would never do again.

"You said investigation was part of why you returned, sought me out at the masquerade," he said at last. "What was the other?"

Her lips parted at the question. She hadn't expected him to pursue it. She hadn't even been fully cognizant of saying it. But now that she had and he was…

"Because I didn't want to walk away from what we shared those two nights," she whispered, her voice barely carrying in the quiet room. "I-I couldn't, even though I knew what I was doing was wrong."

He didn't respond, just stared at her. His face was unreadable now. Not angry, not contemptuous, just...blank. Cool.

"My uncle is going to arrange a new marriage," she explained, somehow unable to keep the words from cascading from her lips. "I'm certain it will be like my last."

"What was your last?" he bit out.

Heat flooded her cheeks. "With an older man, a union for position, not passion. It was the lack of the latter that took me to the masquerade in the first place. Just to...see that passion. Just a little. And then you touched me, and suddenly it was a flood of passion. A wave that swept me away."

"And so you stole my ability to chose what I would do in order to fulfill your own desires," he said.

When he said it that way, she saw it for the violation that it was. And she hated herself for it. "Yes. I-I did. And it was very wrong of me. I wish I could take it back."

"Do you," he said, and he stepped forward.

The space between them closed in that long stride. He was almost touching her now, invading her space, his warmth curling around her like it had when he'd taken her to his bed. His breath steaming over her. His eyes boring into her.

She held those eyes, remembering what they'd looked like when he wanted her. Seeing a shadow of that same expression even now in this heated, emotional moment. And words fell from her lips without her ordering them to do so, "What would you have chosen if you had known?"

His cheek twitched again, but this time his expression was not of anger. It was something else. Something she had seen before, just the moment before he touched her, took her, in that hidden room at a forbidden masquerade.

She saw it and she knew what he would do even before he pressed his lips to hers. There was nothing gentle to the kiss. She still felt his anger in the way he demanded with his tongue and his hands that closed over her forearms and tugged her even closer.

But she felt his desire, too. She tasted it on his tongue as he drove it hard into her mouth. There was no denying that passion she had come to crave. No denying the man who inspired it so deeply inside of her. She made a soft sound in her throat and lifted on her tiptoes to get closer to him. Her tongue met his and the kiss deepened, widened, crashed like waves on the shore. Destructive and beautiful all at once. She wanted to be swept away.

He swore and broke away from her, setting her aside as he lifted his hand to his mouth like he'd been burned. He stared at her for a beat, two, until it felt like forever. Then he turned on his heel and walked away, leaving her alone in the chamber.

Alone and breathless and utterly confused.

CHAPTER ELEVEN

Matthew entered his study and closed the door behind himself. How he had gotten here, he didn't know. Everything had been a blur from the moment he stepped away from the heated temptation of Isabel's kiss to the moment he was currently in.

He'd left the Callis home, found his carriage, come back here...but the details of those actions? Indistinct at best.

Details of the kiss? Crisp and sharp and playing on a repeating cycle in his dizzy mind. Their background was a drum beat of guilt and shame.

He'd always been able to measure his emotions. He'd had good role models for that in his beloved parents. He didn't let passions rise, he held them in check. Even when Angelica died, he'd turned his feelings inward, keeping them to himself because the world was bound to go on without him. Without her.

But now all that ability to control himself felt lost. All the feelings, the desires, the betrayals bubbled up, and with a curse, he swiped his hands across the top of his desk and sent papers and quills and ink bottles scattering on the floor around him. It wasn't enough.

He thought of Isabel, looking up into his eyes. In a mask, then unmasked, with her uncle, then only with himself. He thought of how he wanted to run from her as far and as fast as he could, but also how he wanted to pin her against a wall and fuck her like a wild animal. His head throbbed with all the overwhelming and discordant desires and he strode to the sideboard. He poured himself a drink and lifted the glass to his trembling lips.

He downed it all in one gasping gulp and then pivoted to throw the glass against the wall. It shattered with a very satisfying sound, one that almost seemed to lessen the riotous emotion in his chest. He threw the next, then the next, and was about to throw a fourth when the door to his study flew open and revealed his butler, Portman, and behind him, Baldwin.

Matthew slowly lowered the glass to his side and looked around the room as they did the same. The destruction was clear and he was certain his own emotions were, too.

Baldwin stepped inside, but held up a hand to stay Portman. "That will be all for tonight."

Portman looked past him, his face lined with concern. Matthew turned away from it, from the trouble he had created both in this room and in his life. He heard the butler murmur something to Baldwin and then the door shut.

"You left the party," Baldwin said, his tone very careful. "It was obvious you were in a great upset. And I was the one sent to ensure you were well."

Matthew laughed, though he felt no pleasure. "Is it not obvious? I'm right as goddamn rain."

Baldwin sucked in a long breath. "Once upon a time, I might have expected this kind of reactionary behavior from say...Graham, or maybe Lucas? Perhaps I'd still look for it in Hugh given his mood of late. But in my friend Matthew? Never. So something very bad must have happened at that party, and I'm demanding you tell me what it is right this moment."

Matthew faced him at last. Baldwin's face was tight with worry. An expression he had not seen on his friend's countenance since before he married Helena the previous year.

"You didn't abandon your bride to come seek me out, did you?"

Baldwin arched a brow. "Don't try to distract me, it isn't going to work. Helena was just as worried about you as the rest.

She stayed behind and will be escorted home by James and Emma. She does not expect me back until morning, so you have plenty of time to stop dancing around it and tell me just what the hell is wrong with you."

Matthew sagged and leaned heavily against the sideboard. "I have this one glass left. Drink?"

"Certainly, we can share it. Pour, sit and talk." Baldwin marched across the room and sat down in a chair before the fire. He kept his dark gaze focused on Matthew, who poured the drink, and settled in place across from him, handing over the glass.

"I don't know where to start," he said softly.

Baldwin tilted his head. "I know you saw Fenton Winter at the ball tonight. Did he speak to you? Make the same old accusations as he's been repeating for three years?"

"No," Matthew whispered. "I did see Winter and it did upset me, as it always does. But it's not him. It's...*her.*"

"Angelica?" Baldwin said.

Matthew tensed. *Her* had always been Angelica, from the moment he'd carried her limp body from the lake and his life had been blown to bits. She was the *her* he brought with him to every corner of his life.

He'd assumed she always would be. But tonight, now, the *her* was very different.

"No," he ground out. "I'm talking about my swan. My stranger."

Baldwin's eyes widened, and he looked around the room at the destruction once more. "A woman you hardly know inspired...this?"

"I saw her tonight," he admitted, tilting his head back against the chair and closing his eyes. "I know who she is."

Baldwin caught his breath. "Who?"

Saying it out loud was not going to be easy. It forced him to relive every bloody moment of that night all over again. "She is...Isabel Hayes."

"Who?" Baldwin asked again. "I don't know that name, nor

why it would inspire all this in you."

"She's Angelica's cousin. Fenton Winter's niece and his fucking houseguest."

Baldwin was utterly silent and Matthew waited a moment before he looked at him again. When he did, his friend's face was pale, his mouth dropped open in shock, his eyes wide as saucers.

"Yes, that was my reaction, as well," Matthew drawled, and reached out to snatch the glass from Baldwin's hand. He downed half of it before he handed it back. Baldwin drank the rest, his hands shaking as he did so.

"I-I don't even know what to say, what to do with that information," Baldwin said at last. "It cannot be a coincidence, can it?"

Matthew got up and went back to the sideboard. This time he returned with the bottle. He filled the glass and then took a swig from the bottle itself before he set it on the floor next to his chair.

"I dragged her off to a parlor to confront her about just that. And I was…cruel."

Baldwin drew back. "*You*? Not that I don't think she deserved a little cruelty after she deceived you, but I have a hard time imagining it."

"Just like you have a hard time imagining me destroying my study in a fit of rage and…well, other things?" Matthew asked, flicking his head toward the damage behind him. "Of course I wasn't physically hurtful. Though I'm sure she must have felt threatened. I was…coarse. I'm never coarse. But I was overwhelmed."

"I'm sure you were," Baldwin reassured him. "After all, she knew your identity, did she not?"

Matthew nodded. "Though she insists it wasn't until after my mask slipped off the first night we…" He shivered. "I would say *made love*, but that isn't exactly accurate, is it? I didn't make love to a stranger in a mask. I took her. Claimed her. Burned something into her, just as she burned something in to me. And now I know that the person I did that with is my fiancée's cousin. A woman who lives with a man who would shoot me through my heart if he had a chance."

"Are they in league?" Baldwin asked.

Matthew drew a long, ragged breath. "That was my guess. He despises me, blames me, though he's been quieter about it in the last year or so."

"Doesn't mean he isn't still nursing his hate," Baldwin said.

Matthew sighed. "And what better way to get to me than through Isabel? But she said not."

"Of course she would," Baldwin scoffed. "To protect herself."

Matthew found his fists tightening in his lap. There was a flare of protectiveness that he didn't want rising in his chest. Something Isabel surely hadn't earned.

And yet...

"She seemed sincere in her terror on the subject. She said he couldn't ever know what she did. That she came to me at first because she wanted...it doesn't matter what she wanted. Once she knew the truth of my identity, she came the second time to investigate me. Of her own volition."

Baldwin pursed his lips. "And you believe her?"

Matthew shut his eyes. He could see Isabel so clearly now, those big, dark eyes holding his. Those full lips trembling as she begged him to believe her despite the fact that she had lied. And then the feeling of those lush lips when he claimed them once more. Despite what she had done. Despite what and who she was.

He shook away the thoughts and got to his feet.

"I don't know what I believe," he admitted.

Baldwin nodded slowly. "I think that's fair. To not know, I mean. After all, it's a complicated situation. Perhaps you don't have to know what you believe all at once, when you are overwhelmed by all the aspects of this unexpected development. I think a better question might be, what do you plan to do?"

Matthew moved to the fire and stared at the flames.

Everything had happened such a short time ago. His world had been suddenly flipped, both by the realization of what and who Isabel was and by the fact that it didn't change the pulsing desire he somehow felt for her.

And he hated himself for that. Deeply.

"I don't know that either," he whispered. "My gut tells me that I must stay far away."

He heard those words come from his lips, and immediately they sounded wrong. Staying away wasn't what he wanted. He wanted to dive further into this. To understand her motives more. To try to discover why he was so drawn to her when he had not allowed himself to be drawn to anyone in such a long time.

Baldwin pushed to his feet, oblivious to the thoughts in Matthew's mind. "I understand that," he said slowly. "I even agree it would be for the best."

"Yes, for the best." His voice sounded hollow and far away.

"And it shouldn't be so difficult to avoid this woman. You've done so with her uncle for years. That party tonight was unexpected, but we will all be more vigilant about invitations from now on."

Matthew found himself nodding, but he didn't believe what he was agreeing to. In truth, he had the impression that avoiding Isabel might be harder than his friend imagined. Especially since the coiled desire inside of him turned him into a wolf, more like Robert than any of his other friends.

And that wolf inside told him one thing: to chase her. Not run.

Isabel staggered as she reentered the ballroom, her head spinning wildly and her lips hot and tingling from Matthew's hard and passionate kiss. Her heart fluttered as she scanned the room, but did not find him. Had he left? Was he hiding? Was he going to publicly expose her?

She had not taken two steps into the chamber when her uncle appeared at her elbow.

"There you are," he said, his tone odd and echoing and faraway.

She turned to face him and found he was staring at her with an expression as strange as the tone of his voice. Heat rushed to her cheeks, as she feared she might be showing the strength of her reaction all over her face.

That would not do.

"Hello, Uncle Fenton," she said, her voice shaking. "Were you looking for me?"

"You disappeared from the ballroom," he said.

She swallowed. "I didn't mean to worry you. I went to the retiring room to gather myself. I have a bit of a headache." The lies fell from her lips a little too easily. But then, that was what she was becoming: a liar. Matthew certainly thought so.

Her uncle tilted his head. "Funny, I looked for you in the retiring room."

She froze. If Fenton knew what she had done with a man he so deeply despised...oh, it would be very bad, indeed. He could never know. Never.

"We must have just missed each other," she breathed.

He looked at her more closely. "Yes. Well, if your headache is still troubling you, perhaps we should end our night a bit early."

She nearly collapsed with relief. "Oh, thank you, uncle!" She clasped his arm with both her hands. "You do not know how much I want exactly that."

He arched a brow and looked her up and down. "I shall call for my carriage then. Come along."

He moved them toward the door where she had just entered. She couldn't help but toss one last glance over her shoulder as they left, but found no Matthew within. His friends, all those dukes and their wives, were gathered in a cluster, though, talking and frowning. Had he spoken to them? Did they know?

Nausea rose in her stomach, and she turned away and

focused on making it to the foyer without casting up her accounts. Her uncle called for his rig and she stared at her slippers as they waited, reliving every moment with Matthew in the chamber.

His anger had been so big, it filled the whole parlor. But the desire was still there, too. Like warring factions trying to lay claim to him. Desire had won for a moment, but she feared the rage, the hatred she had inspired by deceiving him…those would take the war. She deserved it, of course, but it still made her heart sink to think that the conversation they'd just shared would likely be their last.

"Isabel."

Her uncle's tone was sharp, and she looked up to find him watching her closely. His expression was unreadable but utterly odd. "Y-yes?"

"The carriage," he said, motioning to it.

She shook her head. "I'm sorry."

She followed him to the vehicle and let him help her up. He took a place across from her and off they went into the night, away from the ball. Away from the moments that had truly changed her life.

"What is it?" he asked.

She jerked her face toward him. "I'm sorry?"

"You are very distracted, Isabel," he said, his tone harsh. "Far more than I would expect from a mere headache."

She swallowed. If she wanted to survive this mess, she would have to learn to cover her reactions better. She forced a smile. "It was merely a very interesting night, uncle. Nothing more."

"Interesting. Yes, I agree. It was a very interesting night." He leaned back against the carriage seat, his arms folded and his gaze still locked on her. "You created a stir, didn't you? Even bigger than I thought you might."

She wrinkled her brow and her musings on Matthew faded. Her uncle's demeanor was so very strange now that her heart began to pound. "What do you mean?"

"Nothing yet," he said with a dismissive wave of his hand. "I must think a bit before we talk about it."

"Think?" she repeated. "Think about what?"

"About your future," he said. "I realized tonight that you might have a much bigger one than I'd originally hoped for. It changes my plans, that is all."

"What do you mean a bigger future?"

"Perhaps a baron or a second son just isn't lofty enough," he explained with a shrug.

Her heart sank and she slouched down in her seat a bit. Here she had been so terrified about her connection to Matthew she'd thought Uncle Fenton could see it. But he was instead focused on that marriage he planned for her. That future she had tried to ignore was rushing toward her despite each passing moment in Matthew's arms.

Now it was almost here. She had to find a way to accept it. And accept that whatever fantasy she had built around Matthew would never be a reality again. Her memories, even the terrifying ones from tonight, would likely be all that kept her warm from this moment forward.

CHAPTER TWELVE

It had been three days since the Callis ball, but to Matthew it felt like a lifetime. The fact that he had hardly slept did not make the moments pass any faster, of course. Nor did the fact that every one of his duke friends in town had come to call on him, to ask him questions. So he'd had to repeat the story of discovering Isabel's identity over and over, reliving it each time.

But the worst, and best, part of the way he'd passed the days were the intruding thoughts about his encounter with Isabel. Kissing Isabel. Isabel lying to him. And touching him.

"Christ," he muttered as he pulled his horse up short in front of Mattigan's Bookshop and slung himself down. He secured the animal to a nearby post and patted the mare's shoulder before he looked up at the building with a smile.

Mattigan's was a favorite haunt of his. When he read, he forgot everything around him. Everything that troubled him. He needed that escape now more than ever, which was why Mattigan's note that a few of his requested books had come in was like a message from the heavens. Matthew was more than ready to forget his troubles.

When he opened the door, the little bell rang and his smile widened. Mr. Mattigan, a portly man of middle age, looked up from his ledger behind the high desk across the room and his face lit up. "Ah, sir, sir, welcome to you."

Matthew came across to him, hand extended, and the shopkeep shook it none too gently in his enthusiasm. "Mr.

Mattigan, I was so very happy to get your message. My books are in?"

"They are at last, and with my apologies in the delay," Mr. Mattigan said with a contrite incline of his head. "The French are most dastardly when separating us from our entertainment."

Matthew laughed. "I think that is overstating it a bit. I think I'll look around a while before I settle the tab and pick up my parcel."

"Of course," Mattigan sat, patting his arm. "Take your time."

Matthew drew in a whiff of the air as Mattigan returned to his place at his desk and took up his pen once more. The smell of paper and ink filled his lungs, and for the first time in days, Matthew was at peace. He stepped toward the shelves and heard the low murmurs of other patrons from down the aisles. Book people. The very best of people, he'd always thought.

He trailed his fingertips along the spines of the books, tilting his head to see the titles of the works, the authors. He'd read most of them, he owned most of them, piled on shelves here in his home in London or out in his far more impressive library in Tyndale. Luckily, there was always a supply of authors, scribbling wildly by candlelight to give him something new to enjoy.

If only his favorites would write faster.

He turned the corner of one aisle into the deeper shelves away from the door. As he did so, he came to a sudden halt, for standing at the end of the shelves of books was Isabel Hayes.

She had not seen him, that much was clear. She was too engrossed in the volume she held in her hands, her eyes wide as she turned a page and reached up to twist a loose lock of hair around her fingertip.

She was exquisite in that moment, and he drank her in. Her dark hair framed that pale, slender face to perfection. There was a sweetness to her lips and an innocence to the way her dark brown gaze darted across the line of words before her. She was utterly engrossed, and for the first time he did not think of her like she was at the Donville Masquerade. There she was temptation and pleasure, sin and seduction.

But the Isabel who stood just feet away from him now was something…more. Still tempting, yes. But also lovely and light. He had the sense that he could settle in beside her and read over her shoulder for a few hours. Or discuss whatever she was so interested in until they had worked out the problems of the world. Or at least the plot holes in the story.

His heart had begun to pound and for a moment, he considered just walking away. Only she looked up at him before he could and their eyes locked. He saw abject terror flit through her entire being. She nearly dropped the tome in her hands, and she pivoted to make her own escape.

"Running again?" he asked.

She froze and then slowly turned to face him. She had not the ability to erase emotion from her face, it seemed, for all her fear and guilt and pain were obvious still. She glanced up at him, fighting for bravery even though her hands were shaking. So much so that he heard the faint rustle of the pages from her book.

"N-no," she whispered, then cleared her throat and repeated the word louder. "No, Your Grace. I was just…stunned to see you here of all places."

He arched a brow and eased closer a step, though he had no idea why he did it. He should avoid this woman, as he had promised each and every friend that he would. But seeing her here, in this place he considered almost sacred…well, he found he couldn't walk away so easily.

"Here of all places," he repeated. "That does not bode well for your judgment of my intelligence."

Her lips parted and she jerked the book up to her chest, almost like a shield. "I-I didn't mean that, of course."

He found himself smiling. Smiling even though he knew she had lied to him. Who she was. What she was.

"What *did* you mean then?"

She stared at the floor with a focus any person would envy. "I only meant that this place is so…special to me. An escape. I was shocked to look up and find you here."

He wrinkled his brow. "That is exactly how I feel about Mattigan's."

Her lips parted and she glanced up. Once again those dark brown eyes held his and he was lost for a moment in chocolaty depths. Pulled back into memories of when those eyes were lit with ultimate pleasure.

"Then you must also understand why I wanted to run when I first saw you standing there," she said.

He leaned on the shelf with his elbow. "I thought you said you weren't running."

She shrugged. "I'm not going to treat you like a fool, Your Grace. We both know escape was my intention."

"And why?" he asked.

"I thought it best," she said. "Considering how you must—"

She cut herself off with a wavering exhalation of breath, like whatever she might say was painful.

"How I must?"

"Hate me," she whispered. "I thought I should leave you alone considering how you must hate me."

Isabel could hardly breathe as she watched Matthew's face transform with her words. It crumpled and then went softer.

"I don't—" He stopped and seemed to struggle for what to say. "Isabel, I was angry when I realized you'd lied to me. When I realized who you were."

She turned her face and tried not to relive that awful moment when he'd confronted her a few nights before. "I'm sorry. I know that is cold comfort and that you don't truly believe me. But I will keep saying it."

He reached out, and suddenly his fingers brushed along the top of her hand. Though they both wore gloves, the electric energy that had flowed between them since that first night in the Donville Masquerade came back in an instant. Her body responded to it, even if she knew it shouldn't.

She lifted her gaze to his and found his gray eyes flitting over her face.

"I was harsh at the Callis party," he said, his voice low and rough. "I was unkind in my upset. And coarse—I said things a gentleman ought never to say to a lady. I apologize for that."

Her lips parted, for in that moment the gentleman had returned. The tender lover. The man who had so captivated her in body—and yes, in soul.

"I don't think I am owed anything," she said.

"*Everyone* is owed a modicum of respect," he said.

She bent her head. "Well, I thank you for that."

For a moment it was quiet between them, and she thought he might make his excuses and walk away, the subject between them closed at last with this less emotional meeting and his final apology.

Instead, he lifted a hand and tapped the book that still drooped in her own. The one she'd almost forgot all about.

"What are you buying?" he asked.

She glanced down at it and then held it out so he could inspect it. She blushed as he glided a finger over the gilded title. "*The Monk*," he said with a grin. "Mrs. Hayes, you are interested in such scandal."

She held out her hand for the return of the book even as her cheeks burned. "I'm certain a gothic tale feels very silly to you."

"On the contrary, I rather like it," he said with a shrug as he returned it to her custody. "It's not the best of its genre, though. I think Beckford is a better representation."

"I agree," Isabel said with a smile. "Though in some ways, even more scandalous. There are certainly more deals with the devil."

To her surprise, he laughed at the quip, and she stared. He was so transformed when he talked about a subject that was clearly a passion for him. A passion she shared. But when he laughed, that transformation was even more complete. He seemed so light in that moment, so separated from the troubles that had weighed him down in the short time she had been acquainted with him.

"Isabel?"

They both turned, and Isabel jolted. She had come to Mattigan's with Sarah, and the moment she had started talking to Matthew, she'd all but forgotten that fact. Now her friend stood just behind them, staring at them with wide, blue eyes.

"Sarah, I'm sorry I got caught up talking to the Duke of Tyndale," Isabel said, trying not to catch her friend's eye so that Sarah couldn't send her messages with her pointed gaze. "Are you acquainted with Miss Sarah Carlton?"

Matthew glanced at her friend. "I believe we've met once or twice. Good afternoon, Miss Carlton."

"Good afternoon, Your Grace," Sarah said. "It is lovely to see you again."

"And you," he said. He cleared his throat. "Well, I'm glad we ran into each other again, Mrs. Hayes."

She nodded slowly. "As am I. Though I doubt it will happen again, so I suppose this is…farewell." She almost choked on that last word.

His expression dropped. "You are likely correct. Good— goodbye."

He inclined his head toward Sarah, then pivoted on his heel out of the aisle. She heard him speaking to Mattigan for a moment, though she couldn't make out the specific words at this distance, and then the bell at the door rang and he was gone.

She sagged against the bookshelf, her heart pounding wildly with the exchange. She'd thought their final encounter had been at the Callis party, when Matthew had kissed her so passionately, angrily. She'd come to accept that fact.

But this was, in some ways, worse. To have him approach her, apologize to her, even though she didn't deserve it. To have him connect with her about the book she was buying, like they were old friends. Like what had happened between them was somehow...*good*...that made it all harder.

"He is very handsome," Sarah said as she slid an arm through Isabel's. "I'd forgotten how handsome."

Isabel snorted out a laugh. "How you could forget is beyond me. It haunts my very dreams."

Sarah guided her from the aisle and toward a pair of chairs Mattigan had placed before the fire in the back of his shop. They sat there together, Sarah searching her face. "You told me he hated you."

Isabel shrugged. "I thought he did. Maybe he still does, he's just too...too *good* a man to show it. Because it isn't right or fair to be cruel to a lady. Even one who deserves such censure."

"You don't deserve cruelty," Sarah said softly. "You sought out passion. Perhaps that isn't accepted in our society, but that doesn't mean it's wrong. And he gave it, freely, accepting that he would not know your identity. What happened after, the connection you two shared even before you knew that you shared a common link in Angelica...that is unfortunate. But you were no more party to that than he was."

"Yes, I was," Isabel moaned as she placed her head in her hands. "I knew who he was and I still went back. I went back and let him...let myself..."

Sarah blushed scarlet. "Yes. I know. I know."

"Oh, it doesn't matter now. He was polite and I appreciated that. But it doesn't change anything. He knows who I am and he wants nothing to do with me. I must accept that and move on. My uncle will demand that I do so, at any rate."

Sarah reached out and took her hand. "I wish I could make it different. For both of us."

Isabel glanced toward the door, where Matthew had departed moments ago. Her heart ached, though it shouldn't. "So do I. But it isn't. And somehow we will both find a way to endure it."

Isabel's body felt heavy as she trudged through the front door into her uncle's foyer. Hicks appeared within a flash and took her gloves before he motioned down the hall.

"Mr. Winter is in the blue parlor, Mrs. Hayes," he said. "About to have tea."

Isabel let out a sigh. At present, she did not wish to see her uncle. He had been so very odd since that night at the Callis party, muttering to himself, getting up and just wandering from rooms without warning. His moods made her nervous and she was already nervous enough about Matthew.

And since she'd seen the duke today, that was all so much sharper. She feared, in some deep part of her, that her uncle might see it. See that connection with a man he despised and suspected.

What horrors would come from that knowledge, she didn't even want to consider, truthfully.

Still, the man was her blood and her...guardian, she supposed was the best descriptor. She couldn't avoid him. It wasn't fair.

She moved down the hall to the parlor and found him standing at the sideboard, picking through a tray of biscuits, a steaming cup of tea already at hand beside him.

"Good afternoon, Uncle Fenton," she said, as brightly as she could muster when her conversation with Matthew still seemed to ring in her ears.

He turned and his gaze flitted over her before he smiled. "Isabel, you have good timing, for you can see tea is served. And I think Mrs. Gooding has your favorite biscuits in the pile. You like the little chocolate ones, do you not?"

Isabel nodded. "I do, indeed. I couldn't have planned it better."

He took his plate and his cup and stepped away from the sideboard. As she poured herself tea, he cleared his throat. "How was your excursion? The bookstore, yes?"

"Mattigan's," she said, adding milk to her cup before she took two of the chocolate biscuits he had suggested. She took a place across from him with a smile. "And it was successful. I left my new book on the sideboard."

He glanced over his shoulder. "Something I'd like?"

She shrugged. "You've never been one for the gothic romances. This one was recommended by a..." She trailed off and shook her head. "By a friend."

He arched a brow, and something in his demeanor shifted. His lips thinned and his gaze flitted to his tea while his brow furrowed. "Hmmm," he grumbled.

She took a deep breath as she examined him closely. She knew that look. He was brooding now, though she had no idea why her talk about Mattigan's would cause him to do so. It wasn't like he had any clue about Matthew's presence there.

"Uncle," she began, and steeled herself for the question she had wanted to ask for months but hadn't had the nerve. Now she steadied it within herself. "Are you...are you well?"

He gave her a look. "Well?" he repeated, like he didn't understand the question.

"Yes." She set her tea aside and scooted to the front of her chair. She hesitated a fraction, but then took his hand in hers. "You've been so troubled these past few years. With very good reason, of course, but it worries me. And in the days since the Callis ball, you've been even more distant and disconnected. Is there something I can do for you?"

For a brief moment, his expression softened. But then that look faded, hardened. He tugged his hand from hers. "I have been thinking a great deal lately about my life. About what and who destroyed it."

Her heart sank. This was an old song. She knew every word to it even before he began. "Oh, uncle," she whispered.

He ignored her. "He did this."

She shut her eyes. In the past, when he had begun to rail about he, him, Tyndale, she had felt nothing but pity. Perhaps a little curiosity. But that was before she knew Matthew. Had spoken to him and kissed him, touched him and so much more. Before she had begun to know, even a little bit, how gentle he could be.

So now when he began to rail, her body and soul responded far more powerfully. There rose up in her a wild desire to defend Matthew.

"Him," she said carefully. "I suppose you mean Tyndale."

"Yes, *Tyndale*," he spat, and glared at her as if she were as much to blame as the very man he despised. "You know he has no honor. No value at all, despite what those in Society think of him."

Her lips parted. "Uncle—"

He pushed to his feet and slammed the cup on the table, sloshing hot tea all over the rim and his hand. He didn't seem to care as he stomped across the room. "Do not defend him. Don't you dare."

She shut her mouth before she foolishly did just that. Say too many good things about the man and her uncle might see what she had to hide. What he could never, ever know.

"I'm going to solve this," he muttered, almost more to himself than her.

"What?" she asked, rising slowly and tracking him as he paced. She didn't understand, for there was nothing to solve, as far as she could see. Angelica could not be brought back. And yet Fenton's face looked almost...calm in this moment. Serene despite his rage. That frightened her more than anything had in a very long time. "Solve...solve what? How?"

"I'm going to destroy him," he said softly. A small smile tilted his lips. "I've been looking for a way to do it for a very long time. A way to get close enough to truly hurt him. And now I know."

She stared. Her uncle's face was red, his eyes glazed with a rage that seemed to almost pulsate through him. He had cursed Tyndale before, of course. Dozens of times. Maybe even hundreds. But this felt...different. This felt serious and real.

"Hurt him?" she whispered.

He nodded. "Just like he hurt my daughter," he said.

She gasped and took an involuntary step away from him.

Her uncle believed Matthew had killed Angelica. If he was to hurt him as she had been hurt, that meant he wanted to…to kill him.

"Please, you cannot—" she began.

He held up a hand to stop her. "You needn't worry yourself, child. This only concerns you in the barest sense."

She shook her head. He had no idea how deeply the situation concerned her. For his sake, for Matthew's, for her own.

"And if you are worried that I have forgotten you, I haven't," he said, the tension slowly going from his face. "We've received an invitation to a ball tomorrow night and I've accepted. From there, the future will start. Perhaps for both of us." He sighed. "Now I've things to do. Have a good time with your book, my dear."

He patted her on the shoulder as he departed the room, and she sank back into her chair once he'd left her alone. Her uncle's increasing rage and unhinged behavior was not going to get better, no matter how she'd hoped that it might change and soften with time.

And it was clear she needed to speak to Matthew about it. She had to tell him that he was in danger. Even if that meant she put herself at risk in the process.

CHAPTER THIRTEEN

"So she was at Mattigan's?"

Matthew sighed and took a sip of his watered-down drink as he looked off into the crowd at the ball. It was Hugh who had asked the question, and his mouth was tight with displeasure as he awaited the answer.

"Yes," Matthew said. "Yesterday afternoon, when I came to pick up my order. And before you ask me a hundred questions, I don't know."

It was Baldwin who tilted his head in question, his dark eyes narrowing. "Don't know what?"

"Anything," Matthew breathed. "I'm torn. Part of me doubts everything about this woman because she deceived me."

Hugh snorted out derision. "Isn't that all that matters? Liars are liars, and once you unmask them you can never trust them again." Both Baldwin and Matthew stared at his sharp tone. One Matthew felt wasn't entirely due to his situation. Their friend shifted. "Has it occurred to you that this woman might have arranged for the meeting at the bookshop? Perhaps she even paid the owner to help her in her schemes."

Matthew drew back. "You've known Mattigan as long as I have. Do you really think he would take money from someone to betray me?"

Hugh folded his arms. "You have no idea what someone would do for money. Isn't that right, Baldwin?"

Baldwin flinched and the color drained from Hugh's face

immediately. Their friend had not long ago been in dire financial straits. It had led to his nearly losing Helena, nearly losing everything. But in the past year solid investments and help from their circle of friends had inched him back toward solvency.

"Not well played, Hugh," Matthew said.

Hugh dropped his head. "I'm sorry. I didn't mean—"

"There's no need to explain yourself," Baldwin said gently. "I suppose I am the best of our circle to discuss the desperation a person feels when it comes to financial need. But Mattigan does well in his business, I don't believe he feels that pinch. Even if he did, he makes a great deal more from our little group of friends than the widow of a merchant could afford to pay. Why would he involve himself in something that would cut off his very nose to spite his face? Do you want to tell us why this subject of liars upsets you so much, Hugh?"

Hugh shook his head, his jaw going taut. "No. I'll get drinks."

He said nothing more, but stalked off into the crowd, leaving Baldwin and Matthew alone again. Baldwin sighed and faced him. "He might be wrong about some vast conspiracy of your lady and the book man, but he isn't wrong to be concerned about you. You said you were torn—does that mean that part of you wants to believe in this woman, despite what she did?"

Matthew nodded slowly. "Yes. I saw truth in her shocked and horrified reaction that night at the ball. And the same when I talked to her yesterday. I have a hard time believing she's a villain. At least not entirely so."

Baldwin pinched his lips together and looked out over the crowd for a moment of quiet. Then he glanced at Matthew again. "You want to believe the best in those around you because you are decent. But I do want you to be careful. This woman, she clearly woke something in you that has been dormant since you lost Angelica. Don't confuse that with a deeper connection. Or allow it to put blinders on you to any ulterior motives she may have."

"You are determined to think the worst of her then?"

Matthew asked softly, feeling a wild desire to defend Isabel.

"Not determined. Just wary. And you should be too. She just entered the ballroom."

Matthew froze, then slowly turned toward the entrance of the chamber. There, across the wide expanse of the hall, was Isabel and her uncle. She was, as always, stunning. Tonight she wore a beautifully cut pink gown with a darker lace overlay that fell over the skirt. Her gaze darted around like a little bird, seeking out shelter in a storm.

For a brief, wild moment, he wished he could provide it. Protect her. Despite the fact that his friends seemed to think he was the one who needed to be guarded.

"I'm going to go find Helena," Baldwin said. "For it is clear you no longer need me. But please, do be careful. If anyone has earned a long life free of trouble, it's you. And if you go in that direction, that is not what you might find."

Baldwin clapped Matthew's arm and then stepped away into the crowd. Matthew found he could say nothing as he departed. His gaze was too focused on Isabel. Perhaps they were right that to avoid her was the best answer.

But he moved toward her regardless, and pushed away all the consequences he knew he might find when he reached her side.

Isabel clung to her uncle's arm as they stepped into the crowded ballroom. Her heart pounded and her stomach fluttered with intense nervousness, something that increased every time she thought of Matthew.

She had no idea if he would be here tonight. For years, he had avoided events where her uncle came, and Fenton had done the same. But now the men were on a collision course, whether Matthew knew it or not. And it was up to her to warn him of the dangerous waters ahead.

She glanced at her uncle. He had the strangest little smirk on his face as he looked over the crowd. One that froze her very blood.

"Why don't you circulate, my dear?" he said as he released her arm. "I have a few friends to talk to, and I'll bring you a refreshment in a while."

She nodded as he walked into the crowd. She had no idea if her sense of dread was a dramatic overreaction or a deep warning she had to head.

"Good evening, Isabel."

She froze at the deep voice that came from just behind her. That voice she knew so well. The one that she wanted to hear and feared in equal measure.

She slowly turned and caught her breath. Matthew. Matthew, so beautiful and fine and perfect as he stared down over her with an impassive expression that she could not read.

"Your Grace," she murmured.

He reached out a hand and she found herself lifting her own, watching as his gloved fingers slid into hers, how he raised her hand with impossible slowness to those lips that had once touched her in the most intimate ways.

"I should not be so pleased to see you as I am," he said, she thought more to himself than to her.

Her heart leapt regardless. But then her mind screamed at her, reminding her about Uncle Fenton and his cruel threats. About all that she had to share with the man who was still holding her hand.

She tugged it away and stepped a fraction closer, dizzy from the warmth of his body as it curled around her. "Matthew," she whispered. "I must talk to you right now."

He wrinkled his brow in confusion. "Are we not talking?"

She shook her head. "Not here. We must talk in private. Please, won't you come with me?"

She saw the hesitation. She hated it, for it was well earned by her decisions and actions. But then he seemed to surrender, his expression softening a fraction as he nodded. "Certainly.

Come, we'll find a place to be alone."

Her body tensed at those words. At the way he said them. It wanted things she should not desire, things she couldn't have. She followed him from the room, knowing full well she had to get these desires under control. Because once he heard what she had to say, it was very unlikely he'd ever want to be alone with her again.

Matthew watched as Isabel entered the parlor and walked as far away from him as she could. He shut the door behind her and shuddered. They were alone. And the space was so small that she could run all she wanted, but it would only take a few steps to have her in his arms.

Which was where he wanted her when he was honest with himself. All his reactions to that ever more evident fact rose up in him. Guilt. Anger. Self-loathing. And desire more powerful and potent than he'd ever experienced before.

Even with Angelica.

And there it was. The truth that he didn't want to face.

Isabel turned, and all those emotions faded to the background. Her expression was taut not with desire, but anxiety. She worried her hands before her, fear lining every part of her lovely face.

"What is it?" he asked, stepping toward her.

She jolted, and her cheeks filled with color. At least he was not alone in this madness. This need that should not be.

Somehow that offered little comfort.

"Has something happened?" he asked, gentling his tone slightly.

"Yes. No. I don't know," she gasped out. "My uncle…"

She trailed off and he stiffened. Fenton Winter. He tried not to think of him. Had avoided him for years. Isabel's presence in his life forced him to bring the man back to the corners of his existence. Him and his accusations that cut so close to the bone.

"What about him?" he asked, sharp and harsh because he could be nothing else.

She lifted her gaze to his. "He is…he's always hated you, Matthew. Blamed you for what happened to Angelica."

He turned away and paced off to the window, where he looked out at the faint shadows of the garden beneath a sky that contained only a sliver of moon. "This is not news to me, Isabel. Certainly it is not something that requires we leave the ball and come here together." He faced her, thinking of Hugh's earlier suggestion that Isabel might be manipulating this situation. He didn't want to believe that.

But…

"But he has been more driven the past little while, Matthew," she said, unaware of the conflict in his mind. "I see a desperation in his eyes. A growing danger. He said that he wants to hurt you."

Matthew shook his head. "He's told me worse to my face, Isabel. It is bluster, pure hatred vomited out by a man deep in grief and loss."

"No!" she snapped, that lilting voice finally going sharp as she closed the distance between them and caught his hands with both her own. "No, it's more than that. I see him on a daily basis, Matthew. I see his deterioration, his descent into something ugly and cruel. At least when it comes to you. You must not take this lightly."

He stared down into her face, lit with true concern and deep fear. For him. For *him*. His friends felt that way, certainly. His mother, yes. But Isabel was the first person outside of his inner circle who had looked at him with such true and deep connection since…

Since her cousin. And he realized how much he had missed the feeling that one soul cared so truly and completely about his own.

It was terrifying and compelling all at once. Something he wanted to recoil from and embrace in equal measure.

"Isabel," he said softly, letting his gaze brush over her lips, meeting her gaze, feeling how she trembled, in part because she believed what she was saying. In part because she was practically in his arms.

"Don't discount me," she asked, her voice shaking.

"I'm not," he said. "I'm certain you believe this is true. But—" He couldn't help himself. He slid a hand along the curve of her jaw, brushed his thumb against her ear and felt her earring bob against the flesh. He watched as her eyes fluttered shut, and she let out a ragged sigh that spoke volumes about what she wanted.

It echoed what he wanted.

"But?" she asked.

He dropped his head down, closer and closer to hers. He felt her breath against his lips, and it drove him mad. "He can't hurt me," he whispered. Then he took her mouth.

She lifted into him at once, her arms coming around his neck as she opened herself to his kiss. And he took. Took like a man starved because he was. He had not kissed her since the ball almost a week before, and then it had been angry and out of control. A punishment rather than a pleasure.

Tonight it was pleasure. It was a memory of steamy nights in that forbidden club when he had lost himself in a stranger. But now she wasn't a stranger, and if anything he wanted more. He wanted to see her whole face as he took her, wanted to feel her body flutter around him in release and whisper her true name against her skin.

He wanted her. Isabel Hayes. And nothing else mattered in that moment except for that one fact.

"Please," she whimpered against his lips. He wasn't certain she meant to say it out loud, or if it was a plea to herself or to him. But it turned his body rock-hard and he found himself backing her toward the wall.

She gasped as her back hit the hard surface, and tilted her head as he started to kiss along her jaw, down her throat, to the low neckline of her pretty gown. She dragged her fingers into his hair, making incoherent sounds of pleasure as he cupped both breasts in his hands, pushing them together, licking the valley that peeked up from her gown.

He ground against her as he did so, hard, circular thrusts of his hips that she met in kind as she gasped and groaned and begged him to keep going. He had no intention of doing anything else. He pushed aside doubt and guilt and recrimination and cupped her backside, lifting her up against him, letting her feel the reminder of what they had shared in secret.

"Yes," she grunted, her fingers digging into his shoulders as she drove her tongue into his mouth and showed him, in no uncertain terms, how much she wanted what he offered.

It would have happened. He had no doubt that it would have. Except in that moment, the door to the parlor opened. He released her, setting her down before he swiveled to face the intruders.

And there, standing in the doorway was her uncle, and he wasn't alone. With him was the host of their party, Lord Hasselbreck, Hugh, and at least three others who were leaning all over themselves to see the wicked, heated scene before them.

CHAPTER FOURTEEN

Isabel gasped in horror at the gaggle of people now staring into the room, looking at Matthew, looking at her. Even half-hidden behind him, she knew her identity was obvious. Especially when her uncle pointed a finger across the room and shouted, "You see! I told you that bastard was up to no good. He is attacking my niece."

Matthew made a sound of utter horror deep in his throat. He cast her one look, and it was no longer the one of desire. The one of need and passion. No, he glanced at her with...uncertainty.

As if he thought she might be part of her uncle's attack.

"No!" she cried out without thinking of the consequences as she hurried around Matthew. "That is *not* what is happening."

That only seemed to make it worse, for the stares of those in the hall became accusatory. She could read the slurs in their eyes. The judgments that she would offer herself so easily.

And from the glare of Matthew's friend, the Duke of Brighthollow, she guessed she would find no friends amongst those who had intruded on this scene between them.

"His Grace was just...I was...we were..." she stammered.

She looked at her uncle then, in some way hoping for help, for support. But he met her stare, then looked past her toward Matthew, and he...*smiled*. A smug expression of triumph. And she knew in that moment. She knew.

When he'd spoken of hurting Matthew, when he'd talked to her about her future...those two things were linked in his mind.

He had planned to use her in this very way. To destroy her if it meant destroying Matthew, too.

"I suggest that everyone leave the room right now," Brighthollow said, spearing those in the hall with a dark glare that could have frozen Hell itself. "Lord Hasselbreck, take them, please. I will remain behind with Mr. Winter and His Grace to ensure they do not come to blows."

Isabel flinched, for at that moment it looked like Brighthollow would not mind raining a few blows down on Uncle Fenton, himself.

"This is my home, Your Grace," Hasselbreck began.

Brighthollow turned his ire on him and snapped, "And I suggest you manage it."

With that he gave Hasselbreck a shove and closed the door behind him, leaving the four of them alone.

Isabel's hands were shaking as she approached her uncle. His gaze, which had been so firm, so celebratory, now fluttered away from hers. A sign of guilt, perhaps, but not so much that he didn't use her as a pawn in this game of his.

"You did this," she whispered, hating how her voice cracked. "You arranged this intrusion, didn't you? For how long?"

Matthew caught his breath and she looked to see him staring at her and her uncle. Both of them with the same expression. Betrayal. Distrust. Her eyes swelled with tears, but she blinked them back. It was too late for that now.

"Answer me!" she shouted.

Uncle Fenton shrugged. "How could I arrange what this person, this *thing*, brought to bear on himself? Did I tell him to pin you against a wall and practically rut with you in public?"

She turned her face at the coarse description. Her stomach turned.

"You have hated me for years," Matthew said at last, his eyes narrowing on Fenton. "What is the purpose of this...manipulation?"

Isabel held her breath as she awaited that answer. Wishing

it would be something that didn't break her heart. Knowing it would.

"You are seen as such a paragon of virtue, aren't you, Tyndale?" Fenton hissed, spittle flying from his lips as he sneered in contempt. "Well, they see you for what you are now. They're talking about it in that hall. How the great, good, decent Duke of Tyndale just flattened a girl half his status against the wall and nearly fucked her. Without benefit of marriage. Without thought to how it would destroy her reputation. No matter what you do now, that will follow you, won't it?"

Matthew wrinkled his brow. "And her. It will follow her—does that not matter to you?"

Isabel stared at him, the uncle she had loved all her life. A man she had mourned with and trusted. A man she had tried to save from his darkest impulses.

And walked into a trap where she was bait.

"He doesn't care," she whispered, and frowned as a tear slid down her cheek. She wiped it away and turned her back on all three men. She could not face them. Not when they all thought so little of her.

The room was silent, heavy, and then Matthew let out a sigh. "You must have known more than what you say."

Brighthollow stepped forward. "Matthew," he began.

Matthew held up a hand to silence him, his gaze still fully focused on her uncle. "Being caught in such a compromising position would tarnish my reputation, of course," he said. "You win on that score. But you must have also known what I would be forced to do next."

"What's that?" Fenton's tone was sing-song. Mocking. Isabel gripped her fists against her legs, leaning over slightly as she was overcome by dizziness and nausea.

"I'll arrange a special license," Matthew said, his voice flat and dark.

She spun around, her eyes wide, her heart throbbing so hard she feared it could be heard by all in the room.

"Tyndale!" Brighthollow shouted, crossing the distance

between them in a few long strides. He caught Matthew's lapels and shook him. "What the hell are you doing?"

Matthew shrugged away, smoothing his coat as he looked not as his friend, but at her. His expression was utterly blank. Utterly distant, like she was someone he didn't know.

"What I must," Matthew said softly. "You saw their looks, Brighthollow. By the time we leave this room, this story will have spread to every corner of that chamber and out into the world. It will multiply and change until what we were caught doing was far worse than the truth. There's no other choice but to do what is honorable."

Brighthollow lifted a finger in her direction. He did not look at her, but he pointed, his hand shaking. "*She* does not deserve to be saved by you. She was likely part of his plot from the first moment it was hatched."

Isabel turned her face, but she didn't respond to the accusation. At this point, there was no reason to do so. Matthew would believe what he did. Thanks to her uncle's deception, why would he think anything but exactly what his friend accused?

And if that kept him from making a mistake she knew full well he would regret, then so be it.

"You are looking out for my best interests," Matthew said at last. "And I love you for that. But I will not base the level of my behavior on the wrongs of someone else. That is not how a man of honor behaves."

"As if you would know anything about honor," Fenton muttered.

Matthew glared at him, and then he said, "The special license will be arranged. I will tell you when it is done and we will choose a date right away for the wedding. Come, Hugh, I'll need your help."

Isabel stared as the two men moved toward the door. He was saying he would...*marry* her. Marry her as soon as possible. For honor, if nothing else. For honor, even though he suspected her of a betrayal far deeper than when she'd merely kept the truth of her identity from him.

Brighthollow stepped from the room, but at the door, Matthew stopped. He looked over his shoulder, his gaze meeting hers. Then he shook his head and walked out without so much as another word for her.

As soon as he was gone, she buckled against the back of the closest chair. Fenton had the gall to look pleased.

"You knew?" she whispered. "You knew, or else why would you arrange for us to be found in such a manner?"

He glanced at her and some of his glee faded. Under it was now at least a flash of guilt. But also anger. Directed at her.

"I knew you were sneaking out," he said. "Doing something I guessed you ought not. But you were a widow, not an innocent, and I had no energy to chase after you and force you to guard what you would not protect of your own volition. But it was not until the night of the Callis ball that I understood the depth of your secrets."

Her lips parted. "The Callis ball."

He nodded and took a step toward her. "I didn't know that bastard was there. I avoid his company whenever I can, but he must have been a late addition to the party."

She folded her arms, trying not to go back to that night when Matthew had uncovered the truth and confronted her. And kissed her. And made her want him all the more. Just like he had tonight.

"I turned and there he was, lurking around. Pretending to be the saint that he is not." Fenton's eyes went cold and blank, and it struck utter fear into the very heart of her. "I saw him approach you and I was ready to call him out. I saw him haul you from the room and I raced to your rescue. But by the time I found the parlor you were in, you were already in his arms. Kissing him like a wanton. The man who murdered your own cousin."

She lifted her chin. "I don't believe he did any such thing, uncle. There has never been any evidence about the night Angelica died except that it was a terrible accident."

His jaw set. "He killed her and you fell into his arms like it was nothing."

She huffed out a breath of frustration and pain and fear, mixed together in the worst possible combination. She stared at him, trying to find the man she'd known all her life beneath this thing he had become after years of festering grief.

"Are you saying you hatched this plan of yours that night?" she asked.

He jerked out a nod. "The seed of it was planted, yes. And it grew as I realized you two were more connected than even I realized."

She shook her head. "What are you talking about?"

"That day at the bookshop. I followed you. I know you met with him. I saw you talking, heads so close, through the window."

Her stomach turned. "You were following me?"

He shrugged. "You have very little call for outrage, my dear. After all, I was only a concerned chaperone, wasn't I? Looking out for my dear charge as I should. At least that is how the world will see it."

"You look out for me by exposing me to the gossip that will follow. By revealing me in the worst light possible."

"It is what I must do. In fact, I will encourage the worst of the rumors, remind people of my old suspicions that have been dismissed all this time. I will make that man a pariah, I will make him a scandal."

He looked so pleased, he looked so satisfied, and Isabel couldn't keep the tears from her eyes this time. One slid down her cheek as she stepped up closer to him.

"And me," she whispered. "You would destroy me to hurt him. You would put me in the path of a man who you truly believe killed your daughter."

His face fell a fraction and he turned it away from her. "Sacrifices must be made, my dear. But don't worry. This won't go on for long."

He turned away and she stared at his retreating back, horror gripping her at his last declaration. "What does that mean?"

"Come, there is much for us to do. A wedding to plan," he

said over his shoulder.

"Uncle!" she called out, but he ignored her, too driven by his plan to pause or consider her. "Uncle!"

He was gone, down the hall, heading back to the ballroom where he would say God knew what in order to stir the pot of rumor and scandal.

With a shudder, she sat down in the nearest chair and covered her face. When she was a girl, she had pictured getting married. Books had given her the fantasy that she could find true love and happily ever after. Reality had been very different. She'd accepted it once, she'd been ready to accept it again after this brief period where passion had reigned.

But now…now she would marry again. This time to a man who not only stoked a fire deep within her, but one who did not trust her. Probably didn't even like her.

A man who was being forced to the church at the tip of a spear.

This was how she'd marry. And she would have to protect him against all the attacks her uncle was about to launch. Even though he didn't want her.

Matthew sat in Ewan and Charlotte's parlor, a drink in his hand. He could hear voices in the hall, murmuring his name. Hissing Isabel's. And he sighed as the door opened and his friends and their spouses marched in.

"This is ridiculous," he said, setting the drink aside as he rose to greet them. "It's the middle of the night—no one needed to be pulled from their bed to deal with me, Hugh."

He looked at the faces of his friends, drawn and concerned, and rolled his eyes. This was going to be a longer night than it already had been, and his head was throbbing.

"Are you going to tell them what happened or am I?" Hugh asked, his tone as dark and angry as it had been since the moment he had dragged Matthew from the party and back to Ewan and Charlotte's home.

"I'm tired of explaining everything," Matthew said, waving his hand at Hugh. "You might as well tell the story this time."

"Fenton Winter has enacted some kind of revenge plot on Matthew at last," Hugh spat. "And he arranged for him to be caught in a compromising position with that niece of his, Isabel Hayes. The two of them have hatched a plot for Matthew to wed her. And he has agreed to it."

There was a collective gasp that moved through his friends, and Matthew flinched at the sound. Flinched as all of them started talking at once, shouting out questions. He let it go on for a moment, then raised a hand.

"Enough," he said, and the cacophony didn't grow quieter. "Stop!" he said louder, more firmly.

They stopped talking at once, exchanging looks with each other, pity and worry, fear and regret. He hated it all. He remembered it too well from all those years ago when these same men had rallied around him after Angelica's passing. It was both a comfort and a vice around his heart.

"It is true that Winter arranged for a dramatic moment tonight, where Isabel and I would be caught," he said softly. "But what was happening in that room when the door opened was no one's fault but my own."

He flashed back to those moments, of Isabel's mouth on his, her body pressed between him and the wall. Her soft moans of pleasure as he treated her with an animal lack of control. That was not him. It never had been. But the moment he touched her it became...feral.

"My apologies to the ladies in the room," Robert said, stepping forward. "But isn't it possible this woman manipulated the scenario? To...trap you?"

Matthew bent his head. Just as it had always been from the first moment he realized who Isabel really was, his thoughts on her were complicated. Of course it was possible that she was in on the betrayals of her uncle. He knew that—he was no fool.

After all, she would benefit greatly from a marriage to a duke. Many a lady had attempted the same thing in many a closed parlor.

And if she still suspected the same thing her uncle did, despite the hesitations she had expressed to Matthew in the past, she might even be willing to sacrifice her reputation to avenge the cousin she'd clearly loved.

The idea that nothing between them had ever been real turned his stomach. And yet, it wasn't the only feeling he had. He remembered the look on her face when they'd been interrupted. The wavering shock in her voice when she confronted her uncle. The way she had thrown herself in front of Matthew and denied that she was being accosted.

"I don't want to believe that. I want to believe that she is just as innocent a party as I am. After all, she asked me to come to the parlor to warn me."

Now it was Lucas, the Duke of Willowby, who moved forward. He had spent years as a spy for the government, and in that moment it showed on his face, which was suddenly hard. "Warn you?" he repeated.

His lips parted. "She was trying to tell me that her uncle wanted to hurt me. I played it off. You all know how long he's been railing against me, declaring I should be destroyed for what he thinks I've done. But it seems he has made good at last. And this is his first step in some larger plan."

Lucas's wife Diana reached out to take her husband's hand. Her expression was just as troubled as the others, despite her being the newest addition to their group. "You think there is danger."

"I don't know," he said. "Perhaps. And if Isabel is truly an innocent in Winter's plans, then that danger might extend to her, as well."

His stomach tightened. He already knew what it was like to lose someone he cared for. He had experienced the pain of screaming out someone's name and getting no answer from the limp body in his arms.

He never wanted to repeat that. Never.

"So you will marry this woman," Charlotte said, resting her hand on the swell of her belly she shook her head sadly. "Oh, Matthew."

He shrugged. "There is nothing else to do about it. Not after what happened tonight. He has forced my hand, and now it must play out. I'll arrange for a special license tomorrow and have the wedding as soon as possible."

James, Duke of Abernathe and long the leader of their group, grabbed for Matthew's arm. "Don't rush this, Matthew."

"I must," he said, staring into his friend's eyes. Seeing the pain James felt for him. "For her sake, for my own. At least it will remove Isabel as a pawn in his game."

"Or put her squarely in position to take everything," Hugh snapped. "You are a fool if you consider her a pawn and not an all-powerful queen on the board."

Matthew flinched. It was easy to think of Isabel as a queen, in truth. Just not the kind who would come into his world and destroy it. And he could only hope he was correct in that assessment.

"I appreciate the concern and the pitying stares and all that," he said to the group at large. "But this is happening now. And the best thing you can do for me is to just support me in it."

"Or course," Baldwin said, reaching out to squeeze Hugh's arm before he offered a hand to Matthew. "Congratulations, my friend."

There was no denying the mournful tone of Baldwin's voice, but Matthew took the offering. They shook, Baldwin's eyes holding his steady and true. He nearly buckled beneath the support. And when the others came up to offer the same, he felt their strength and their love flowing through him, buoying him as it had so many times before.

"It's the middle of the night," James said when everyone had taken their turn. "I suggest we all go home and regroup tomorrow."

"Yes," James's wife Emma said as she took his arm. "It will

look better in the morning, it always does. Come along, everyone."

Matthew smiled as the group said their goodbyes and filed from the parlor in a buzzing line. In the end, it was only Charlotte and Ewan left. Charlotte let out her breath in a long sigh.

"I'm sorry, Charlotte," Matthew said. "I had no idea Hugh would haul everyone from their beds in an emergency meeting. You need your rest and it was unfair."

Her brow wrinkled. "You think I do not fully support this impromptu gathering of the 1797 Club?" She shook her head. "You took my mind off my child kicking me all night at any rate. So, I thank you for that."

She glanced at Ewan, and a world of unspoken communication flowed between them. She signed out a few little movements of her hands, the language of love the two of them had developed over years of friendship and longing and then true and powerful love. Ewan smiled briefly, then leaned in to kiss her cheek.

"I leave my husband to reassure you further," she said as she took Matthew's hand. "Goodnight, my dearest friend. As sweet Emma said, it will be better in the morning."

"Good night," Matthew murmured as she left the room.

He turned to find Ewan observing him closely. Reading him, as his cousin had always been able to do. Normally he didn't resent the almost brotherly ability, but tonight he felt raw and he didn't want Ewan to see that.

He was glad when Ewan broke his stare and pulled out the little notebook from his pocket. He scribbled a message and handed it over.

"Do you feel anything for her at all?"

Matthew tensed. That was the question, wasn't it? The one he was trying to avoid answering because he didn't fully know it. But here, with Ewan, he could be honest in that.

"Desire," he said softly. "In spades. It wasn't her who started what happened in that parlor tonight. It was me. When I'm near her it is…fire. I've never felt anything like it."

Ewan nodded, as if he understood. Matthew assumed he did. He'd certainly caught glimpses of plenty of passionate kisses and hidden moments between his cousin and Charlotte since their marriage.

But there was still trouble lining Ewan's expression. *"Desire is a start,"* he wrote. *"But I'm asking how you feel."*

"Conflicted," Matthew choked out. "How the hell am I supposed to marry Angelica's cousin? How the hell am I supposed to figure out the truth from all the lies that started out between us? Is she the swan I seduced in a hell? Is she the manipulator Hugh is certain she is? Is she the girl in the bookshop who blushes over gothic novels? Who is she?"

Ewan considered that a moment, then wrote, *"She may be all of those things. You are more than your grief, are you not? Or your desire? Or your friendship with our group?"*

"This is why I don't talk to you," Matthew said with a little smile. "You are so rational."

"Talk to Robert for irrational," Ewan wrote. Then he frowned. *"Or Hugh, as of late."*

Matthew let out a long breath and bent his head. "This was not the plan, Ewan. This explosion that just went off in my life was not the plan."

"The best things start that way. Now, is there anything I can do?"

Matthew read the note with a smile and reached out to squeeze his cousin's shoulder. "Just...be you. Supportive and watching. Kind and so damned logical." Ewan didn't smile in return, and Matthew sighed. "He's got me trapped now. Until we see why, that's *all* you can do."

CHAPTER FIFTEEN

Matthew straightened his jacket as he stared at his reflection in the mirror. He looked…tired. Wasn't that what everyone had said to him over and over again during the two days since his surprise engagement? The one that would be completed tomorrow thanks to a special license, hastily received after the exchange of copious amounts of money.

There were benefits to having power. Only he felt powerless.

Powerless to this marriage that was hanging over him. Powerless against the tide of desire he felt for the woman who would be his bride. Powerless against whatever plans Fenton Winter had in store for him.

He shook his head and glanced over his shoulder as his chamber door opened.

"Mama," he said, turning to face her with the best smile he could muster. It felt as false as it likely looked.

Her smile was just as untrue. "You do look handsome, my love," she said as she came up to squeeze his hand.

They stood together for a long moment, and then he sighed. "I know you are…troubled. Just as everyone is troubled."

"I won't deny that. I think any mother would be, given the circumstances. Winter has hated you for years—no amount of reason could change his mind about what he believes you did. I have never understood it."

Matthew looked at his reflection again as he considered that statement. "I do."

She drew back. "You do?"

"When Father died," he began, feeling her stiffen. Her fingers tightened in his. "You don't know how I wished I could blame it on someone, something. The pain was so sharp, so strong, I would have loved to place it somewhere else. Focused it into anger or hate. To lose a child...I imagine that would be a thousand times worse."

She nodded slowly. "Yes, I suppose that is true. Anger feels like it is more controlled than grief. More purposeful. But still. To go so far..."

He shrugged. "Well, he did go so far. There is no escaping it now. And in the end, it was my own actions that placed me into a moment he could capitalize on, isn't it? Had I not been so imprudent..."

He waved his hand rather than complete the sentence. Whenever he did, he was yanked back to that moment in the parlor when Isabel had been flush against him and all reason had failed him, replaced by something hot and hungry that took control.

"What is she like?" the duchess asked.

He turned toward her. "Isabel?"

"Your friends seem quite...*divided* on the subject."

Yes, his protective friends, half of whom saw Isabel as a co-conspirator, the other half as a victim. He wasn't sure which camp he fell into.

"She is lovely, of course," he began. "You could not help but look at her across a room. But the closer one gets, the more...fascinating she becomes. She's intelligent, which I like."

"You would be bored to tears if she weren't, so that makes me happy," his mother said.

"And she has a sweetness to her. She was poorly matched before, you know. In a loveless marriage."

She bent her head. "And now you will both be thrust into another. Not what I ever wanted for you, especially after watching your friends and your cousin marry so happily. I always wished you would find a union like—"

She broke off, but he knew where her mind was going. "Like yours with Father," he said, sighing. "Yes, I hoped for that too. But you know, it isn't so very terrible. I am drawn to her. There is much to separate us, but there is no reason that one day we could not have a good…a good friendship."

"Perhaps that will be enough," she whispered, her voice cracking slightly.

He lifted it to his lips for a brief kiss. "May I ask you a favor?"

"Anything," she said.

"Lead in the way in how you manage her," he said. "Please. It will be hard enough for her for a while and I don't want her to feel she is under attack from all sides."

"You do care about her well-being," the duchess breathed, tilting her head to examine his face a bit more closely.

He shifted beneath the interest and nodded. "I do."

"Then I will do everything in my power to make her feel welcome," his mother said. "But Matthew?"

"Yes?"

"If she does turn out to be in league with her uncle, I will cut her to her knees."

Matthew lifted his eyebrows at the sharp, forceful tone. His mother was generally so kind, so gentle. And yet now her eyes flashed with the same protective light that his friends had demonstrated.

"I understand," he said.

"Your Grace?" They both turned to find Portman standing in the entryway.

"Yes?" Matthew asked, though he already knew what the butler would say. He just needed an extra breath before he faced it.

"Mrs. Hayes has arrived."

Matthew glanced at his mother. "Only Mrs. Hayes? Mr. Winter is not also here?"

Portman shook his head. "No, sir. Mrs. Hayes came alone.

She is in the blue parlor, as requested."

Matthew nodded, and after Portman had gone, he looked at his mother. "Is it very wrong that I'm happy her uncle didn't join us tonight?"

"No, for I feel it too and I absolve us of all guilt," she laughed as they left the room together to join Isabel. "Though I do wonder at his behavior."

Matthew pursed his lips. "As do I. As do I."

They came down the stairs and up the hallway. The door to the blue parlor was closed as they approached and he made himself take a cleansing breath before he pushed it open and revealed their guest.

Isabel was standing by the window and she pivoted when they entered, her hands clenched before her and her eyes wide. She was beautiful, as she was always beautiful. Tonight she wore a pretty blue silk that made her seem at home in the room. A fall of butterflies adored the skirt of her gown, and the whimsical element made him feel like he was home in Tyndale, lying in the fields like he had done when he was a boy.

When everything was so much simpler.

"Your Graces," Isabel said, hands fluttering much like those butterfly wings when she stepped forward.

"Mrs. Hayes," his mother said, breaking from him and holding out her hand when Matthew could not move toward her. "Or may I call you Isabel, since tomorrow we shall be family?"

"Of course, Your Grace," Isabel said, glancing at him. "I would be honored."

The duchess cast him a quick look over her shoulder. It was pointed, and he realized he had simply been staring since he entered the room. As she stepped away to pour them each a drink, Matthew came forward at last.

"Good evening, Isabel," he forced himself to say.

"Matthew," she whispered, her gaze flitting over his face. "I'm so happy you invited me tonight. I thought you would not wish to see me."

His heart lurched at the breathlessness in those words and

the pain in her gaze. Despite his hesitations about her motives, he still felt a powerful drive to comfort her. To do far more than that. He reached for her hand.

When their fingers intertwined, there was a jolt of awareness that went through him. As always, desire was there. But something else, too. Something he could scarcely put a name to, for he hadn't felt anything like it for a very long time.

It was a feeling of coming home, which could not be correct. He was overwrought after all the excitement of the past few days.

"We are to marry, Isabel," he reminded her softly. "I could not avoid you if I wished to. And I don't wish that."

She nodded slowly, though his words didn't seem to help ease her discomfort. In truth, he had no idea how to do so. They were both thrown into a situation out of their control. They were both aware of the barriers and the difficulties.

She cleared her throat as his mother returned. "My uncle sends his, er, regrets that he could not join us. He was distracted by some business."

From the tightness around her lips, he could see that was not a true statement, and his stomach turned. Was she lying because this was part of some larger plan? And if not, if she were as much a victim as he was, just how bad things were for her at home, with a man so driven by hate that he would sacrifice her for it? Both questions left him ill at ease.

There were voices in the foyer then, and they all turned. "Ah," the duchess said. "The others are arriving. Shall we greet them?"

She smiled at Isabel and then stepped from the room. Matthew held out his arm and she took it. But before he drew her into the hall, toward his friends and the night ahead, he leaned down closer.

"You are beautiful," he whispered.

She jerked her gaze up with a gasp. Like she didn't believe it. Like he couldn't feel it after everything.

"S-so are you," she stammered.

He found himself smiling as he guided her from the room. And for the first time in days, his heart actually felt light.

Isabel stood alone on Matthew's wide terrace, looking down at a shadowy garden below. She could not see much of it in the moonlight, but she could already tell it was massive. Lovely. And after tomorrow, hers.

That thought was shocking every time she stumbled upon it, and she gripped her hands tighter on the metal railing as she gazed into the night.

The past few hours had been...trying. The supper was wonderful, of course. The company fine, for Matthew's friends and their wives were all good people. Decent men and women.

But she saw the way they watched her. Careful. Accusatory in some cases. They were a tightknit group. She had no place there. Not yet. Perhaps not ever.

And that stung even though she deserved no less than their censure.

"He is like a brother to me, you know."

Isabel turned to see Helena Undercross coming across the terrace toward her. The Duchess of Sheffield, Baldwin's wife. And there was no mistaking the hard edge to the otherwise beautiful woman's countenance.

"I know he and your husband are very close," Isabel said carefully.

"They are. All the dukes in their little club are close, but there are pockets of deeper friendships within their ranks. Baldwin, Ewan and Matthew are one of those pockets." Helena stopped beside her and stared up at the stars for a moment. "That alone would make me protective of him. But there is more to it than that."

Isabel tilted her head. She wanted so much to know more about the man she would so soon marry. And this woman, with her accusation, was offering her a glimpse of just that.

"What is it?" she asked carefully.

Helena sent her a side glance. "He would have saved me."

"Saved you?" Isabel repeated, not understanding. It was obvious Baldwin and Helena were deeply in love, just like every other couple in that group of friendship inside. She could not imagine Helena ever would have required saving from Matthew.

"There was a moment when it seemed Baldwin and I would not be able to wed," she explained, her voice shaking as if the mere words cut her deeply. "And Matthew offered to take my hand to help me escape a bad situation."

Isabel's lips parted as she stared at the woman beside her. The very beautiful woman. Alluring and exotic, since she was an American. The idea that Matthew had ever considered marrying her made Isabel's jealousy flare.

"I see," she whispered.

"I'm not sure you do," Helena retorted, facing her suddenly. "And I'm not sure how I feel about you in return. There are things about you that make me want to offer you friendship. But I doubt you, Isabel. And I fear what that doubt means for Matthew."

Isabel swallowed. Thus far no one had been so direct about their hesitations. She found she almost appreciated it, though the confrontation was not a pleasant experience. At least it was straightforward.

"I understand your hesitation," she said. "And I know my words will mean little if I do not match them to action as time goes by. But I will tell you that I do not want to hurt Matthew. Right now you may not believe that, but in time I hope you will."

Helena tilted her head, and some of the hardness went out of her face. She let out her breath slowly. "So do I, Isabel. So do I."

Matthew stepped onto the terrace and came to a stop. Isabel was there, starlight falling over her like she had been conjured from some fairy story. Or a gothic tale like the ones they had discussed together at Mattigan's.

But with her was Helena. And by the way the two women were looking at each other, there conversation was very intense, indeed.

"Ladies," he drawled.

Helena backed away a step and turned to him with a smile. "Matthew."

"The others have left and I believe Baldwin was just saying farewell to my mother."

Helena nodded. "Then I should join him." She faced Isabel again. "Thank you for your candor. Good night."

"Good night," Isabel whispered, her voice barely carrying.

Helena walked away, toward him. She caught his hand as she passed by and squeezed it gently. "Good night."

He kept his eyes on Isabel as Helena went inside and shut the door behind herself. At last they were alone. Alone for the first time since that night when their future had been sealed.

He should have wanted to pepper her with a thousand questions and accusations. But that wasn't what came to his mind at all. No, watching her standing at his terrace wall, her hands shaking, her eyes not meeting his, what he wanted was to fold her into his arms. Comfort her. Touch her.

He shook his head. "You survived the night," he said.

She jerked her face to his. "There were times I wasn't certain I would," she admitted. "There are half a dozen friends of yours ready to place a knife between my ribs if I dare to ever hurt you."

He pursed his lips. "They are protective. I'm sorry."

She looked back over his garden. "You ought not to be. It's nice to have friends with such loyalty."

"You do," he said. "Sarah Carlton seems to be such a friend to you."

There was a shadow of a smile that crossed her lips. "Yes.

And I suppose one benefit of our union is that I would be able to help her."

"Help her?" Matthew repeated, fascinated by the moonlight dancing off her dark hair.

She faced him. "Yes. She's in a dire state. Once her mother is gone, she will likely be forced to go into service. And perhaps with the influence of your title, I can help her a little as she transitions."

Matthew wrinkled his brow. His friends had their own ideas about this woman's ulterior motives when it came to their marriage. But here was one, and it was something he could not fault. He had the same instinct to help his friends at all costs. To use what influence he had to improve the lives of those he loved.

Another thing they had in common.

"I think we could be of help when that time comes," he said. "I hope you'll turn to me for assistance."

Her expression softened a bit. "If you would be willing, I would greatly appreciate the help."

He reached out, for he could no longer resist it, and touched her cheek with his bare fingers. She sucked her breath in through her teeth and leaned into his hand as her eyes fluttered shut.

"Isabel," he whispered, just to hear her name out loud.

"Matthew," she murmured back.

He leaned in and kissed her. Her hands trembled as she lifted them to cup his cheeks and draw him even closer. Her lips parted beneath his and he took what she silently offered. The kiss deepened, grew more heated. He knew where it was headed.

He couldn't allow it. Yet. Not yet. Not here, not with his mother just through a door.

He pulled away reluctantly and she sighed out a tiny sound of displeasure.

"You and Helena had a talk?" he asked, searching for a topic that would distract him from the very hard cock rubbing the front of his trousers at present.

She nodded. "She is certainly protective," she murmured. "But I suppose she would be. She—she told me you once offered to marry her to save her from a bad position."

Matthew jolted. He had not expected Helena to share that particular tidbit. It had been a year before, a moment that felt worlds away now. "Not because I cared for her. At least not beyond friendship," he said, feeling he should explain himself. Not certain why.

"You don't owe me anything," she whispered.

He shook his head. "We are to marry. Tomorrow. So I think I do. Baldwin was in a bad situation. So was Helena. They believed they couldn't be together and so I offered to marry her myself, to save her. I mostly did it to make Baldwin wake up to what he truly wanted. He did, they married and all is right between them."

She pressed her lips together. "Indeed, it is. All your friends are remarkable in that way. Those that are married appear deeply in love. Powerfully."

He turned his face, for this felt like a dangerous topic. Very dangerous, indeed, considering how many of those same friends had struggled just as he was struggling. Many of them had experienced a reluctant courtship, driven by desire. A blossoming of feelings that not a one of them expected. And then…the magic of the lives they now shared.

That was not his path, but he found he increasingly envied it, especially as he looked at the beautiful woman before him.

"I will have to prove myself with them," Isabel said. "To prove I am not in league with my uncle. I suppose I'll have to prove that to you, as well."

Matthew shifted at that particularly unpleasant thought. The one that had been haunting him for days. He cocked his head. "Speaking of your uncle…"

"You want to know why he did not come tonight?" she asked. Her cheeks darkened. "He made a show of getting ready, rubbing his hands together, talking about making scenes. And then, just as suddenly, he said he would not come. That he did not want to step foot into your home until it was absolutely necessary."

She let out a long sigh, and in that moment he saw how exhausted she was by this exercise. By her uncle's swinging pendulum of moods and what it had wrought on her life. He also saw her fear, the same one she had expressed to him the night they had been caught together. What he didn't see was any kind of deception. Perhaps he couldn't fully trust himself, but he didn't think that Isabel was lying to him.

"If he could have come here and caused trouble, but didn't, that must give you some modicum of relief," he said.

Her eyes widened. "It doesn't."

"Why?"

She shook her head. "His eyes are still so wild, Matthew. I feel him plotting with every turn, muttering beneath his breath about having you close enough to hurt. Why don't you take it seriously?"

He reached out and caught her hand. They both looked down at their intertwined fingers. Watched as he lifted her hand and pressed it to his chest. Her fingers tightened there, like she was trying to hold his heart. For a wild moment, he wished she could.

"You've lived with him a year, yes?" he asked. "Well, I've endured this behavior from him three times that long. He blusters, but he does not act. Right now he's reveling in how he created a scandal surrounding my name. Perhaps that will finally be enough for him."

She didn't look certain, so he leaned forward, sliding his fingers along her jaw once more. Whatever words she'd been going to say fell away as her breath caught and her eyes fluttered shut.

He brushed his lips to hers, gentle this time despite the animal instinct that rose up in him once more. He drew her closer, against his chest, folding his arms around her. She shivered as she settled there and in that moment he felt something entirely new. Entirely unexpected.

He felt peace.

She pulled away and looked up at him, expression bleary

and almost confused. Like she, too, had felt that shift and it took her off center just as it did him.

"We marry tomorrow," she whispered. "I can hardly believe it."

He nodded. This would be the perfect time to pull away from her embrace, but he didn't. He continued to hold her as he said, "It's happened very fast."

"And what will happen…a-after?" she asked.

His jaw tightened at the question. It was one he had been pondering himself. That vast blankness of what their relationship would be as husband and wife was troubling to say the least. And now she had asked him to put voice to it.

"I don't know," he admitted. "I don't know what will happen, but I know what I want when you're near me like you are right now. Despite everything."

Her brow wrinkled. "Despite," she repeated, and there was no mistaking the faint hurt in her tone. He wished he didn't cause it, but didn't see a way not to. Not right now, at least.

"Despite is all I have, Isabel. You cannot fault me for that, can you? After all the lies and manipulations that brought us here."

It was she who pulled away, taking a step back from him as she stared at her hands clenched in front of her. "No, I cannot fault you. If I were to believe you were a villain bound to trap me, perhaps all I would have is despite, as well."

He frowned. She acted as though she felt something deeper for him. Worse, the idea that she did was not the anathema it should have been. He didn't want her heart, of course. That was not something he had ever expected to desire again from a lady.

But if he held it…that was certainly a gift.

"Tomorrow will come soon enough, Isabel," he choked out. "Why don't we just see what it brings rather than wrapping ourselves in knots wondering about it?"

Her lips pressed once more and then she nodded. "That's a fair suggestion, Matthew. I can't say otherwise."

"Good." He held out his elbow. "Why don't you let me take

you back to your carriage then?"

She stared at the outstretched arm for a beat, then slid her hand into the crook of his elbow. He found himself drawing a breath of relief as she did so. He led her from the terrace, back into the house and toward the foyer where he was certain his mother was waiting to say goodbye to Isabel. His fiancée.

Tomorrow, his wife.

And once that happened, everything would change.

Despite a long drive across the darkness of a London night, Isabel's head was still spinning as she arrived at her uncle's home half an hour later. She stared through the carriage window at the house, just another in a row of the same houses, and sighed.

Inside was a man she loved. Still loved, despite his wild accusations and even wilder actions. And he was bound and determined to hurt Matthew. Despite what her fiancé thought, she still believed Fenton had deeper plans than a mere scandal and a forced wedding.

And she was terrified of them. Determined to do anything she could to protect Matthew. Because...

Well, she wasn't going to say the because. Not to herself and certainly not out loud. Her feelings for the man had increased since that first shocking moment he had appeared out of the crowd at the Donville Masquerade and stepped between her and her attacker.

It seemed she was destined to break her heart over him. And sooner rather than later.

The footman opened the door and she climbed out into the cool night air, drawing a cleansing breath before she walked up to the house and into the foyer. Hicks asked about her night as he took her things and she smiled through it, ready to just go up to her room and go to sleep. If she could with the knowledge that in a few short hours she would be Matthew's wife.

"Goodnight, Hicks," she said with a smile for the butler as she moved toward the stairs. She had not yet reached them when she heard her uncle from across the foyer.

"How was it?"

She froze, hand hovering above the banister. She did not wish to discuss her night with him. Her anger and resentment toward him was growing exponentially and she had no interest in engaging in a row with him.

"Answer me, Isabel," he said, his tone sharpening.

She spun toward him, and the anger she'd been trying to keep in check now bubbled to the surface. "If you're going for humiliation, you have hit your mark. Everyone is talking."

Her uncle's face lit up in triumph and she took a long step toward him.

"That makes you happy, does it? Well, it shouldn't. No one is talking about him. They're talking about *me*." She folded her arms. "From strangers in the shop to his own friends and mother. They all look at me like I'm a snake who slithered into their flowerbed. And the reason? Because I am. Because of you. And he—"

She cut herself off, for the last thing she wanted was to debate the topic of *him* with her uncle. Not when her feelings for Matthew were so tangled and powerful and painful.

"He?" Uncle Fenton encouraged.

She shook her head. "Do you want me to say he's miserable? That he's broken?"

"Is he?"

"He isn't exactly dancing in the streets over our union," she said, thinking of Matthew's offer that he could want her despite. *Despite.* Fenton's lip curled up in a sneer, and she shook her head. "You *are* happy about this."

"Why shouldn't I be? He's created enough misery, why should he not feel even a fraction of the same?"

"Good, then you've succeeded," she said, moving forward to catch his hands. "Celebrate as you've always wanted to do.

It's time to let this go."

His face twisted. In that moment she saw all his grief, all his deep and abiding pain, all the loss that had piled up on his shoulders and weighed him down. Changed and warped him into the person who stood before her today. And though she feared that person...she also pitied him. And longed to help him see that revenge and rage were not the answer.

"You never lost a child," he spit, his voice shaking as he yanked his hands from hers. "You have no idea what it feels like. So you have no quarter to talk to me about what I should let go or not let go."

He pivoted and walked away, back down the hall. She heard the door to his study slam, loud enough that the pictures hanging in the hallway shook with the force.

She bent her head as tears gathered in her eyes. And this was how she would marry. As a tool for one man's revenge. A tool for another's desire.

And there was nothing she could do to stop either of them.

CHAPTER SIXTEEN

Matthew looked down the long table filled with friends and family. The servants were just drawing away the last of the dishes for a lavish wedding supper and the group talked softly together.

Only it wasn't his friends who drew his eye. It was Isabel, down at the end of the table. The position of honor. The place that had been his mother's up until that very afternoon.

The place of the duchess. Because that's what Isabel was now, thanks to a few murmured promises in the garden hours before. She was his wife. And that fact jolted him every time it was mentioned.

She was seated with his mother on one side and her friend Sarah on the other. Occasionally he saw Sarah take her hand, speak softly to her. Comfort her, it looked like. And Isabel seemed to need the comfort. She was nervous and agitated, her gaze a bit too wide, her hands shaky when she sipped her wine or ate a bite of food.

He wished he could be the one beside her in that moment. That he could rest a hand on her knee beneath the table and meet her eyes as he whispered that all would be well. Even if that was a lie.

His gaze slid farther down the table to where her uncle sat. Fenton Winter had been remarkably quiet during the day. He had given away his niece with only the slightest of snide comments and had been calm for the rest of the afternoon. But now the man downed what had to be his fourth glass of wine in the last hour. His gaze was becoming dazed and narrowed every time he looked at Matthew.

At last Winter rose, that same glass still in hand. He speared Matthew with a look, pointed and ugly. Slowly, Matthew pushed back from his place at the head of the table. He needed to be on his feet for the barrage clearly to come. At least it was being done in front of only friends, rather than the public displays of vitriol Winter usually displayed.

"Killer," he hissed, wine sloshing from his glass.

James threw his napkin on the table and moved to rise, but Matthew held out a hand, motioning for him to stay put. The last thing he needed at present was for anyone in his large group of friends to call this man out. Deserved or not.

"Oh, you aren't going to say anything, are you?" Winter continued, looking around the table at the outraged faces of dukes and duchesses alike. "Mark that, Your Graces. Would an innocent man not come to his own defense? Ask yourselves why he doesn't do so."

"You've had enough, Winter," Matthew said softly. "Perhaps it's time to go. Go home and sleep this off."

Winter pushed his chair back with a screech that made every single person in the room flinch. He staggered as he came away from the table. "Sleep off what? The truth? You'd like that, wouldn't you? If I would go away and stop reminding you of your guilt."

Matthew shook his head. "Trust that I am perfectly capable of remembering my guilt without your help, Winter."

"Well, now you have a new bride," Winter said. "Perhaps you can find some new guilt there. You'll take my niece like you did my daughter."

"That's enough!"

Matthew jolted as Isabel threw her chair back. It flipped and skidded away. She crashed toward her uncle, an avenging angel with her eyes lit up with emotion.

"Stay out of this, girl," Winter muttered, not looking at her.

"It doesn't concern you."

She laughed, but it was a harsh, cold sound. "You made it my concern when you involved me in your vendetta. We are here, uncle, because of *your* manipulations. You were so blinded by your own rage that you were willing to sacrifice anything to create even a tiny bit of pain in this man's life. Even me." She caught her breath and Matthew saw that she was struggling with tears. "So if you think he is a killer, then what does that make you, that you would hand over your own flesh and blood to him so that you could make him squirm?"

Her uncle shifted and he glanced at her at last. "I won't let him hurt you."

She shook her head. "The only one who has hurt me is you. Now this is my house. You made sure of it today when you marched me up the aisle to a man who did not deserve your machinations. And since it is my house, I have the right to tell you to get out."

Winter flinched and turned on her. "Isabel—"

She pointed toward the dining room door. "You are not welcome here. Not if you are going to accuse my husband of such terrible things. Not if you are going to humiliate him in front of his friends and our family."

"So you take his side," Winter growled. He moved toward her, and Matthew rushed around the table at the idea that he might touch her. But he didn't. He only leaned in. "I am your family. Angelica was. Where is your allegiance?"

She recoiled, but then she lifted her chin. In her face, Matthew saw her power and her strength. Something she normally kept quiet, but was there in all its glory in that charged, painful moment.

"If you were my family, you would have thought of me before you did what you did. And Angelica is dead." Matthew and Winter flinched at the same time. "No one can bring her back, no matter how much you or Matthew wish you could. So I owe her nothing more than my grief that she did not get to live out her dreams. Now as I said, it is time for you to go. And until you are able to apologize and reflect on what you've done, you are not welcome here again."

Winter stared at her, sputtering. Then he cast a deep glare in Matthew's direction and stormed from the room. The chamber sat in stunned silence for a moment as Matthew gaped at Isabel. The fire had gone out of her now, replaced by regret. Pain. She had done this for him. In front of everyone he loved, she had taken a side and it was his.

"Brava!" Graham Everly, Duke of Northfield, suddenly called out as he rose to his feet, clapping his hands. Slowly, all his friends joined in the applause.

Isabel dropped her gaze from his as bright color filled her cheeks. Although they meant well, although he saw that her strenuous defense of him and censure of her uncle had softened more than a few hearts to her, it was clear she was uncomfortable with the accolades. He moved to her and caught her hand, squeezing it as he met her eyes and held them in a show of solidarity and gratitude.

"Enough, you lot," he said, laughing to soften the mood. "This is not a play."

It was Graham's wife Adelaide who grinned at that. She had once walked the boards herself, in a very different life. "If it had been, it would have been lit very differently." She stood and came around to embrace Isabel. "You were very brave. But I can see how tired you two must be after all the excitement of the past few days. I realize a wedding party would normally last a few more hours, but I suggest that we leave the bride and groom to themselves."

She looked around the room with a pointed gaze. Matthew rolled his eyes. She had very little subtlety and yet he appreciated the gesture. In truth, he did want to be alone with Isabel now. His...wife. He shook his head at that reminder of what had transpired hours before.

"Well said, my love," Graham said as he joined his wife. He shook Matthew's hand, his bright blue eyes holding Matthew's for a moment. Offering the support and friendship

Matthew had always known from this group of friends. He appreciated it even more now than ever before.

The rest got up, shaking hands, kissing Isabel's cheek. They all moved into the foyer to say their farewells. He noted that Isabel was quiet during it all. She smiled as she was acknowledged and accepted the friendliness that was offered to her, but she still held herself back. Cautious, as though she didn't trust in this new world she found herself in. And why would she? One couldn't expect change overnight. And there were still so many questions to be answered. By her, and perhaps by him.

At last it was only his mother who remained in the foyer as the carriages drove off into the night. She turned toward them with a soft smile. "You know, my marriage to your father was arranged," she said. "And over time, we came to care deeply for each other. Love each other." She blinked at the tears that always accompanied talk of the late duke. "So I wish with all my heart that despite this complicated beginning, you two will find happiness together." She stepped up to Isabel and took both her hands. "Welcome to our family, my dear."

She leaned in and bussed Isabel's cheeks gently. When she backed away, Isabel smiled. "Thank you, Your Grace. I hope to one day prove that I belong here."

His mother's smile faltered a fraction, and she met Matthew's eyes for a brief moment before she waved her farewells and went to her own carriage.

As she pulled away, Hicks closed the door and turned to them. "Is there anything else I can provide, Your Grace?" he asked.

Matthew looked at Isabel. Tonight he only wanted one thing, and it wasn't anything the butler could provide. Only the woman who refused to look at him. "No. You and the rest of the staff should have a well-deserved night off. Her Grace and I will be fine."

Hicks inclined his head and then glanced at Isabel. "Many felicitations, Your Grace. I hope you and His Grace will have many happy years together and that this home will be a comfortable one for you."

"Thank you, Hicks," she whispered.

Matthew frowned. It was like she was shrinking. Since her confrontation with her uncle, she had grown quieter, hunched smaller. Like she was trying to disappear. And he didn't want that. Not at all.

"Come," he said, offering his arm. "Let me show you your chamber, Your Grace."

To his surprise, she flinched at the title, but took his arm and let him lead her upstairs. He guided her to the door to his chamber and opened it, revealing the drawing room. He saw it through her eyes as she gazed around. It was a masculine space. He'd changed and updated it when he inherited, and now it was all him. He would have to allow her to change that, to bring some of herself into the world he'd lived in alone for so long.

"It's lovely," she said, stepping away from him into the room. "The mahogany furniture is exquisite."

He smiled. "There's more of it in my bedchamber, if you'd like to join me there."

She turned, her eyes wide and her breath short. For a moment, it seemed like she was struggling to find words. Then she simply nodded.

He opened the door and motioned her in. When she passed him into the room, he caught a vanilla whiff of her hair and shuddered with desire. How he had resisted her since the last time they made love weeks ago, he could not say. Right now that felt like an exercise in impossible control.

Tonight he would not exert it any longer.

She moved around his chamber, her hands shaking as she looked at the miniatures on his table. He and Ewan, portraits his mother had done when they were boys. His mother. His father.

Then she turned and faced his bed. His big, comfortable bed that felt so bright and ready in the firelight. She reached out and touched the coverlet, dragging her fingers along the soft cotton fabric with a shiver.

"I am nervous," she said at last.

He wrinkled his brow. "We have done this before, you know."

"I know. But when we did, I wore a mask. And there weren't so many questions between us. Just the desire, nothing more."

He frowned. He wasn't so sure she was right about that. There had always been questions between them. And always more than desire, even though the truth of it was hard for him to accept.

He stepped forward. "Would it make it easier for you if we talked about some of those questions before we...proceed?"

She jerked her face up and met his eyes. The moment between them seemed to stretch for an eternity and then she nodded. "If you want to ask them, please do."

He cleared his throat. A thousand things rushed up in his mind, a thousand facts and lies he wanted to sort out. But the one that fell from his lips surprised even him.

"Why did you come to the Donville Masquerade?"

Isabel blinked at the question. She'd thought he'd ask about her uncle or her cousin. Or talk to her about the uncouth outburst she had created at his table not twenty minutes before.

"That is what you want to know?" she asked. "We have talked about it before."

"But as you said, when we did you wore a mask. I'm not asking Miss Swan. I'm asking Isabel now. I'm asking because I want to know about *you*."

She let out a sigh. "Very well. Though it isn't a very interesting story."

He arched a brow. "How a gentlewoman ended up in a sex club in the underground? I think it is."

She laughed despite the discomfort and uncertainty of the situation. Matthew had the unique power to do that, to bleed out some of the tension that always seemed to rise between them. And to make her comfortable when she ought not to be.

"My husband was very...old," she began. "You know that, we've spoken of it before. My father wanted me to marry a man with means and position in our little Society, and Gregory had both. But he was not...gentle with me. Or caring. It was a flip of my nightgown and a few half-hearted grunts and that was all. Sometimes I got a flutter of something more, of some pleasure, but if I wanted that, I had to find it with my own hand. In secret."

She watched as Matthew's jaw set in anger. Not at her, she didn't think. At her late husband. And why not? Matthew was a man who always tended to her pleasure before he thought of his own. In his mind, a man who only thought of himself was entirely ungentlemanly.

"You were alone, despite your marriage," he said softly.

"Yes," she said, her voice cracking with the painful truth of that statement. "And then he died. He'd been sick all along, but it was sudden. And I was free. Except not. Within a month or so, his heirs from his first marriage swept in and pushed me out. My uncle took me in."

He stiffened. "For his own purposes?"

The question made her ponder that. Right now it was hard to recall if Fenton had always had his own goals in mind. But when she pushed past her pain, she could remember.

"Just as you are not what he thinks, he is not entirely what you believe," she said gently. "He was very kind when I came to him. We could talk and spend time together. I tried to make him laugh, though I failed more often than I succeeded."

She shook her head at the wave of sadness that overwhelmed her with those memories. Where had that man gone? Had his desire for revenge taken him entirely? Or was he still inside the shell of her uncle?

"You were happy there." There was no censure in Matthew's tone. She was glad for it. After all, he had every right to judge her uncle and her.

"I was, for a time. But the longer I stayed, the more he

mentioned that one day I would marry again. That he would arrange for something. Something that would benefit me. Only I knew the kind of benefit he meant."

"Financial. Positional," Matthew said.

She nodded. "After months of a little freedom, I was slapped in the face by the prospect of another loveless, empty marriage. And I was terrified. I couldn't sleep, I used to roam the halls, and that's when—"

She cut herself off, for the next part of her story was the most scandalous of all. She'd never stated it out loud, not even to Sarah.

"Tell me," he said, and he closed the distance between them. He reached out and took her hand, his warm fingers massaging her palm. Perhaps he meant it to be comforting, but it was not that. Arousing was a better word. As his thumb caressed her palm, she felt her body grow heavy and wet.

She swallowed. "I was up in the middle of the night and I decided to find a book in my uncle's library. When I opened the door, I-I saw them."

His eyes widened as her meaning became clear. "Who?"

"A maid and a footman. They were...they were doing all the things that people do at the Donville Masquerade. It was animal and powerful and passionate." She shook her head. "I had never thought it could be like that. But I couldn't stop thinking of it. Fantasizing about it in the dark of my room. I crept down every night, looking for them. Watching them if I caught them. I knew it was wrong, but I just couldn't stop."

His pupils dilated. She knew that look. What she told him made him want her. And that gave her a little bravery in this sea of inappropriate confession.

"The last night I saw them together, he said something about the Donville Masquerade. And then my uncle fired the maid and I never saw them together again. I asked around and ultimately found out exactly what the masquerade was. Intrigued, I snuck out and went. It was shocking to me, of course. But it fueled even more drive to go, to see, to explore that passion that I'd never felt and believed I never would feel. Until…until you."

He lifted a hand to touch her face, his thumb tracing the line of her jaw. It was electric pleasure. It was anticipation of oh, so much more to come. And she was ready. Ready for this, even if it was all they would ever share. It was better than nothing. Wasn't it?

It had to be.

"You deserved that pleasure you sought," he murmured. "And I'm glad I was there to give it to you."

She shook her head. "It's a funny thing, isn't it? That of all the hundreds of people who flow through that place, you and I found each other?"

CHAPTER SEVENTEEN

Matthew's jaw tightened, and for a moment Isabel thought she'd said something wrong. His reaction was so physical and so strong. She opened her mouth to ask him about it, to apologize for going too far.

But before she could, he dropped his lips to hers and her thoughts and fears faded away. At least for now, she could surrender, give herself completely and know that this man—this marvelous, giving man—would tend to her every need. And she to his.

He glided his hands across her cheeks as he tilted her head for better access. His fingers slid through her locks, bringing pins raining down on the floor around them. Her hair fell around her shoulders and his hands, and he drew back to stare at her.

"You've never had your hair down with me," he said, touching the locks like they were something magical.

She laughed. "I suppose not. It's just hair."

"No, it's silk and satin," he said, lifting a piece to his nose and inhaling deeply. "It's midnight and magic. It's vanilla heaven."

She blinked at those words, passionate and sweet. Her dark hair had always seemed too plain to her. But he spoke of it like it was something incredible, so it suddenly felt that way.

She lifted her hands and tugged at his jacket, and he smiled. "Is waxing poetic about your hair is the path to your surrender, Your Grace?" he asked with a grin. "I'll file that piece of information away."

"Silly man," she whispered as she fumbled with the buttons on his waistcoat. "Touching me, saying my name, even looking at me the right way is the path to my surrender. It seems I'm always on the edge of it when I'm with you."

"Good," he growled, suddenly possessive and dark in tone. She liked that. Liked hearing him find his way to animal desire, away from the sweet goodness that normally made itself known.

He suddenly turned her and yanked her back against him. His mouth came down to her neck, and he sucked there as his hand glided to her stomach, holding her flush to him as he ground his hard cock against her backside. She let out a moan at the aggressive touch and pushed back, meeting him eagerly.

"I have been waiting for this," he whispered against her skin, the words sinking into her flesh and working their way through her bloodstream.

She nodded, wordless and breathless, and gasped when he pulled at the gown, popping the buttons free and scattering a few to join her hairpins on the floor.

"I'll buy you a new one," he promised as he parted the gown. "You're wearing a chemise?"

She laughed at the deep disappointment in his tone. "Today I'm Isabel, remember?" she said. "Only the swan goes bare beneath her gowns."

"Perhaps Isabel could take a page from the swan's book from time to time," he said, pushing the dress forward to droop around her waist. He slipped a finger beneath her chemise strap and inched it down her arm. "For me."

"For you?" She gasped as his mouth followed the trail of the strap. "Yes, Your Grace."

He murmured a moan against her skin and then turned her to face him. He locked his gaze with hers and dragged her chemise away. She was bare from the waist up, and heat flooded her cheeks. It was a funny thing, for he was right that he'd seen her like this before. He'd been far more intimate with her body.

But the mask had offered protection. Anonymity. A barrier.

Tonight there were none, and as he stared she turned her eyes away.

He tucked a finger beneath her chin and turned her face back. "Don't. Don't hide from me."

She swallowed hard and nodded, watching him as he watched her. His gray gaze swept over her body, drinking her in, his pupils dilating and his hands lifting to touch her bare skin at last.

He cupped both breasts, sweeping his thumbs over her already hard nipples. She threw her head back in pleasure and he leaned down to suck one peak into his mouth. He worked her tender flesh, stroking and laving, then sucking until she was gasping and groaning his name over and over.

He repeated the same action against her opposite breast, all the while inching her gown and chemise the rest of the way down her body until she was naked but for her sheer stockings.

He pulled away at last, his lips wet from tasting her, and motioned to the bed wordlessly. She smiled as she followed that order, settling back against his pillows and watching with great interest as he stripped his own clothing away.

She sat up straighter as he peeled his shirt off and kicked out of his trousers. He was already hard, his cock curling toward his stomach in a proud display of desire. She licked her lips as she stared at it, anticipating every moment they would share. Every way he would pleasure her.

"You will kill me with just a look," he grunted as he crawled over her, bracing his hands on either side of her head and letting his hips lower to hers so their bodies touched at last.

She hissed out a breath at the heat of his skin against her skin. His hardness on her softness. She had missed this so very much. Thought she'd never experience it again.

And here they were, with the rest of their lives to explore each other. To dive into the well of passion and pleasure together. Perhaps that would be enough. She lied to herself that it would be as she gripped the back of his head and drew his lips to hers.

He sank into her with a shuddering sigh that seemed to move through his entire body. She wrapped her arms around him, cradling him as she parted her legs and created a place for him to rest. He broke the kiss, resting his forehead to hers as he positioned himself at her entrance and then slid effortlessly into her waiting and willing body.

They both exhaled a long sigh, their breath mingling in the quiet. He smiled at her and she massaged her fingers against his back. It felt so right, this moment. No longer stolen, no longer thick with lies. It was their moment and she refused to share it with anything or anyone else.

"Ready?" he whispered, his voice rough.

She nodded. "Oh yes."

He thrust then, long, heavy motions that seemed to take a lifetime. She rose to meet him with each one as she kissed his neck and his chest and his arms. Already, she was on the edge, the result of such a long time apart.

And he knew exactly how to take her over that edge. He ground his hips hard against her, and the pleasure that had been building deep within her reached its peak. She cried out his name as she came, milking him with her quivering body. His neck strained as he took her harder, faster, losing his finesse, losing his control. She watched him as it happened. Watched the moment that there was only animal need driving him. Then he made a guttural cry and she felt him pump hot into her.

He collapsed on top of her, his breath coming short as he smoothed his hands over her naked, sweaty body. She turned into him, kissing him while their bodies were still connected. The moment would be gone shortly and she wanted to make it last. Last as long as she could. Maybe even last forever.

Matthew lay in his bed, watching as dawn's first light began to brighten the horizon out the window. He had not slept that night. Not even for a moment. All of it had to do with the woman beside him.

He glanced down at Isabel. She was tucked into his chest, her hand resting there. Her legs tangled in his. Her naked body half-uncovered after a night of making love to her over and over again. Until she was spent. Until she was incoherent with pleasure. And somehow his desire for her had not been slaked. It was still there, pulsing through him even when he brushed a lock of hair from her forehead and she snuggled closer with a faint whimper of his name.

It hadn't just been making love to her that kept him from sleep. It was the feelings that doing it created in him.

He had every reason in the world to doubt the woman in his arms. The short time they'd known each other had been thick with lies, with manipulations. And yet as he held her, he didn't focus on those things, even if he should. What he felt was a connection. Something powerful that transcended the physical bond that was obvious the moment they barely touched.

This was deeper. It gave him comfort. It gave him peace. It gave him hope.

At least he thought it was hope. Hope had been such a stranger to him lately that he hardly recognized it. He only knew it was powerful and positive.

And when he acknowledged that, what followed was intense guilt.

How could he feel this way about another woman, *any* other woman, but especially Angelica's own cousin? A person he would have met, even invited to his home if his fiancée hadn't died all those years ago. Did that mean he would have betrayed her? That he would have felt this draw to Isabel that now seemed to throb in him like a drumbeat?

What kind of a bastard did that make him?

He let out his breath in a ragged sigh and gently detached himself from Isabel's embrace. She made a soft sound of protest that was lost in the air, and settled deeper in to the pillows. He walked to the window and stood looking out on the garden behind the house.

A new day was almost here. The first of the rest of his life married to Isabel. But he still didn't really know what that meant to him. Or to her. But there was no denying it, just like there was no denying the sun as it finally popped up above the horizon.

So he would have to find a way to move forward.

CHAPTER EIGHTEEN

Isabel paced through the halls of her new home, peeking into parlors and hesitating in music rooms as she explored her surroundings. She spent hours doing so. Well, to be fair, most of those hours had been spent cooing and fawning over Matthew's fine library.

Still, her first day as the Duchess of Tyndale had been occupied, indeed. Just not by her husband, who had been all but hiding since they broke their fast together hours before.

She pushed aside her feelings on that subject and turned into a long hallway. There she stopped. It was a portrait gallery, and her heart leapt. She'd already seen Matthew's miniatures of his parents and Ewan the previous night, little glimpses of the happy childhood he seemed to have experienced. But here she would see generations of the men and women he had come from. She would see his nose and eyes and smile on a dozen faces and trace them back to him.

She stepped out and looked up and down the high walls at each portrait. Some were serious faces, some were kind. There were men with medals pinned to their chests and ladies with dogs piled on their laps and children in their arms. She couldn't help but smile at each one and wonder at their lives.

That smile fell when she reached the far end of the hall. There, in a place of honor on the wall, between a portrait of Matthew and another of Charlotte and Ewan...was Angelica.

She did not recognize the portrait. It was not the same as the one that hung in her uncle's parlor as the centerpiece of his shrine to his late daughter. She tilted her head and examined her cousin's face a bit closer.

"Isabel."

She turned and found Matthew standing behind her. He had approached her so silently that she hadn't even realized he was there. But now he stared too. Right at the woman he had loved. The only one he'd ever truly wished to marry.

"She was lovely," Isabel said, returning her attention to the portrait.

"She was," he said. "I had commissioned that as a gift for her, to be given to her after we wed. Of course, it...it never happened."

She flinched at the life he had planned for her cousin. The one Isabel had now stepped into thanks to a series of deceits that hung between them. And questions. So many questions.

"What happened, Matthew?" she asked, voicing the one question that had launched everything between them. Everything her uncle had done.

"That night?" he asked, his tone stiff and cold.

She faced him and found he was standing ramrod straight and looked not at Angelica anymore, but at her. His face was unreadable, his gaze hooded.

"Yes," she said.

"Wondering if I killed her?" he asked, turning away.

She watched as he started down the hall, and a sudden and irrepressible anger that he would dismiss her so callously rose in her.

She pursued him in a few long strides and caught his arm, turning him to face her by sheer force of will. His eyes went wide. "*No*," she snapped. "That *isn't* what I'm saying and it is unfair of you to accuse me of such a thing and then walk away. You seem to forget that my life has been blown apart, just as yours has. I have a right to wonder why."

He arched a brow. "Has it been blown apart, Isabel? You've married a duke. That seems an elevation."

Her lips parted at the cruel jab. At the coldness with which he said it. She released his arm and backed away, shaking her head with every step. "How little you think of me. I already had a marriage with a man who did not desire me. Now I am with one who doesn't like me, let alone want me."

His brow wrinkled. "You think I don't want you? You don't know what I want, Isabel. For weeks all I've thought about is you. Even when I didn't know your identity, I've never felt anything like it. Feral and hot, dangerous. And I hate it."

She flinched and turned her face. "Hate me."

"No, not you." He moved closer, covering the distance she had created. "You enthrall me, interest me, captivate me. You slept in my arms last night and it felt right. And wrong."

She stared at him. She'd never thought he would say these things to her. Passionate things, words that expressed a deep conflict within him. A conflict that gave her hope as much as it birthed pure terror in her soul.

"Answer me this," she said. "Do you *truly* think I created this situation, either to further my uncle's agenda or to improve my own situation?"

He swallowed. "You defended me passionately at our wedding supper, in front of a room full of people. I saw how humiliated you were by having to face off with your uncle in that forum. But there are times I just…don't know."

She moved closer and lifted trembling hands to his face. He let her touch him. When she did, he let out a low and ragged sigh. Like he'd been waiting for this moment all day. She had been, too.

"I didn't have anything to do with what he arranged," she said softly, then leaned up to brush her lips to his.

When she pulled away, he stared at her. His pupils were dilated and his breath short and unsteady. Then he caught her hand and dragged her up the hall, past Angelica's staring portrait, into a room that she had not yet explored. Another parlor in a long series of parlors.

He pushed the door shut and tugged her into his arms. She

fell against his chest, lifting her mouth to his hungry one as the heat between them, sharpened by their argument, swelled to an inferno. He tugged at her clothes, unfastening buttons, dragging fabric up and down as he shoved her onto the closest settee. She pulled him down on top of her, fumbling for the placard on his trousers and the cock that strained beneath it.

She opened her legs as he tugged her drawers off and tossed them aside. His fingers found her sex and he stroked there, opening her, spreading the wetness across her as his breath grew increasingly ragged.

With difficulty, she finally freed his cock and took him in hand. One stroke, two, and then he crushed his mouth to hers as he lifted her hips and thrust deep into her body. She cried out at the invasion, sweet and hot and animal. He pounded into her, taking and taking, claiming like it would leave a permanent mark. Perhaps it would. She started to shake as he ground harder, his pelvis stroking hers on every deep thrust.

His mouth crashed against hers, demanding everything she had to give. She surrendered it, only breaking away when an orgasm hit her like wildfire. She gave a keening cry and he echoed the sound as he poured himself deep into her body and then dropped down against her, his hands gently smoothing over her arms, her fingers dragging through his hair.

And in that moment, there was peace.

"Someone should design a settee better suited for such things," Matthew complained as he dragged Isabel half across his body and she settled her head against his chest.

She laughed, the tension that had started between them in the portrait gallery bled away by passion. "That is called a bed, Your Grace. You have a very nice one just upstairs."

"A bed," he repeated. "Fascinating. Perhaps we should move one into every room in this house. Just in case."

She glanced up at him, her expression both laced with humor and interest. "An unexpected design choice that I'd hate to explain to guests."

"I'm certain they would determine the use on their own," he drawled.

She sighed, and for a moment both were quiet. The silence allowed him to relive their earlier argument once more. She had asked him about Angelica and his first reaction had been to push her away. To leave unsaid the painful topic of his last night with his former fiancée. But now, with Isabel's hands smoothing over him, with the vanilla scent of her hair teasing his nostrils, he knew he was wrong to hide the truth from her.

Especially when it had impacted virtually every moment between them since.

He steeled himself and said, "Angelica and I had a sometimes...heated relationship."

She went stiff and looked up. She was working to make her expression passive. "How could you not? You are irresistible and she was stunning."

He shook his head as he realized what meaning she'd put to his words. "No, not like that. Not like...*this*. Of course, I was attracted to her, to be certain, but we—we never, that is to say we hadn't..."

Her eyes went wide as she looked up at him. "No?"

"She was a lady and we were to be married." He shrugged. "To do so seemed wrong at the time. I thought we had a lifetime."

She nodded. "I suppose you did. But if you don't mean heated in that sense, then what *do* you mean?"

He frowned. "She would occasionally get upset when I didn't do as she liked. That was what happened that night. The last night. We were all at the estate in Tyndale and she demanded I go out with her onto the lake. She said something about the moonlight. I was in the middle of something. I considered it important, though to be honest, I don't even recall what it was now." He shook his head. "And she...she..."

"Had a tantrum," Isabel finished, not cruelly but with certainty.

He glanced down at her. It was actually rather nice to talk to someone who had known Angelica so well. He could be direct where he was careful with others. Slowly, he nodded. "I suppose that is what you might call it."

"She did that sometimes," Isabel said with a shrug.

"With you too?" he asked.

"Yes." She chuckled as if the memory pleased her. "With everyone. She was passionate, as I'm sure you know. She was fierce, in both how she loved and how she demanded. Just determined to change everyone's mind to her way."

He smiled faintly. "That is exactly right."

"But she was never...cruel," Isabel continued swiftly. "She was just as likely to use honey to get what she wanted as that big dose of vinegar. She'd smile and please and cajole and suddenly I was an ally on her side. Of course, the next time I needed one of my own, she was the first to jump up and link arms with me. She was a force of nature in that regard."

"She was. And often I gave in, just as it sounds like you did. That night, I didn't. We quarreled," he said, trying to block out the images that had begun to fill his mind. "And a while later her maid came to me to inform me that Angelica had gone out without me. Of course, that was meant to make me follow, and I did, still fuming from the ugly words we had exchanged and her foolhardy devotion to doing exactly as she wished."

He focused, trying to regather himself. It must have taken him a long while, for Isabel reached out and threaded her fingers through his. She squeezed his hand gently. "And what happened then?"

"She was in the middle of the lake by the time I reached it," he whispered. "In this tiny little boat that was only meant for children. And when she saw me, she stood up, to prove to me that she would do as she pleased, I suppose. The boat rocked and...and..."

Isabel caught her breath. Tears had filled her eyes. "It

capsized," she said. "Oh, Angelica."

He nodded. "It was so far out, so far away. I raced to her, fully clothed, pushing through the water. She went under again and again as her gown got heavier and heavier. By the time I reached her, she had been under for a while. I couldn't find her in the dark. I was frantic, diving under to search for her. At last I touched her hand and there was this huge moment of hope. But when I hauled her to the surface, she was limp and cold. I kept saying her name as I took her to shore, but there was nothing I could do. Nothing I could do. She was gone."

Isabel reached up, and it was only when she gently wiped his cheek that he realized he was weeping. For the life he had lost. For the guilt he had carried. For the woman who'd had her bright and vibrant light snuffed out over a foolish fit of pique. Isabel's cheeks were also wet and her eyes sparkled with even more tears. For her cousin, but also for him, he could see. Not tears of pity, but empathy.

"I would have traded places with her, Isabel," he murmured. "You know I never harmed her. I hope you know I never would have. I *did* love her."

She nodded immediately. "I do. I can see it, I can feel it. And I'm so sorry, Matthew. Sorry you endured that loss. And so sorry that my uncle's grief has steered him to blame you. But mostly I'm sorry that my presence in your life is a constant reminder of the future you wanted, the one that was stolen from you that night. Those comparisons must be devastating."

She wrapped her arms around him even tighter, holding him close, and in that moment he realized she was wrong. He did not compare her to Angelica. Somehow, he never had. They did not look alike or talk alike or behave alike. That they were related was complicated, of course. Troubling when coupled with the manipulations and hatreds of her uncle.

But it wasn't Angelica he thought of when Isabel touched him. And it wasn't Angelica he wished to know more about as he lay in Isabel's warm arms. But what to do about those desires?

That was something he was still figuring out.

CHAPTER NINETEEN

Although she had been Duchess of Tyndale for a week, Isabel still had a hard time answering when someone called her Your Grace. That was someone else, wasn't it? Someone raised to take that role, someone born understanding the expectations that went along with it.

She was slower to understand, though Matthew's servants had been kind and patient. And so had he. More than kind, actually. She had expected him to pull away after those first few nights they spent as man and wife. To go back to his duties, and distance would settle between them.

But he hadn't.

In the week since their marriage, he had spent time with her. Together, they were carefully navigating what a marriage between them meant. And the result was...wonderful. They spoke of books and read together, he played the pianoforte while she sang, they took walks in the gardens and in the park. All of it felt...easy. The only tension between them was of a sexual nature.

And that tension was combustible when it finally exploded in a frenzy of hungry mouths and tearing clothes and writhing bodies. For hours, they could explore each other, pleasure each other and then fall right back into the friendship she felt growing between them.

He was trying. Trying to make a marriage with her, despite their bad beginning. And she appreciated that more than she ever could have said.

And yet it still wasn't enough. In her heart, she still knew she wasn't his choice. That Angelica hung in the middle of their life, just as her portrait hung in their hall.

She sighed as she stirred her tea and stared out at the garden behind the house. "Why do you want so damned much?" she muttered to herself. "Why not just be satisfied with the comfort of what you have?"

She didn't get to continue the troubling conversation with herself when Matthew raced into the parlor. She leapt to her feet, for his expression was pale and wild as he looked at her.

"What is it?" Her mind immediately jumped to her uncle and a thousand horrible things he could do to them. Even if Matthew didn't believe he would hurt them, she wasn't so certain.

"Charlotte," he gasped, his breath short. "The baby is coming—I just received word."

Isabel clasped her hands together as her terror made way for joy. Although she felt lingering hesitation from Matthew's friends, they were not unkind to her. And she knew how thrilled Charlotte and Ewan were to welcome their son or daughter.

"What are we waiting for?" she said, grabbing his hand and tugging him to the foyer. "Ewan will need his friends there. Portman, have the carriage brought round right away!"

The butler hustled off to call for the vehicle and Isabel smiled up at Matthew with a tilt of her head. "Are you nervous?"

He nodded. "Of course. Anything can go wrong in these situations, though Lucas's wife Diana will attend to Charlotte and there is no better healer or midwife to be found. I think Meg will also be assisting. Charlotte is in good hands, but I still know what it would do to my cousin if he lost his wife."

She pursed her lips at the desperate expression in his eyes. "Of course you do," she said softly. "More than any other. But we mustn't think the worst. Yes, childbirth is dangerous, but most women come through very well."

The carriage arrived and she drew him toward it. He helped

her up and called out to the driver to take them just a half a mile up the lane to Ewan and Charlotte's home. Any other day, she might have suggested they walk, but Matthew gripped his hands open and shut so nervously that she wasn't certain he would survive the walk.

She smiled at him, moved by his concern for his beloved cousin. And his nervousness on Charlotte's behalf. This was why she loved this man so very much.

She swallowed hard as that errant thought made its way through her mind. Love him. Love Matthew. It was the emotion she had tried to subvert any time it fluttered along the edges of her consciousness. Something she had fought back against with all her might, since she knew it could never be an emotion he returned.

Only there it was. Clear and lovely, perfect and true as she stared at him looking out the window, his hands shaking in his lap. She loved him. Deeply and truly, madly and sweetly. There was no doubt she always would, despite…just despite.

They pulled up short in front of the estate and Matthew climbed down, offering her a hand to help her. He was obviously distracted as he took her up the stairs and smiled at the pale servant who immediately took them to a parlor up the stairs and into the private quarters of the home.

As they entered the room, Isabel couldn't help but be pleased. Already the group of these dukes and their wives were milling about. Meg and Diana were just down the hall with Charlotte. Isabel could hear the Duchess of Donburrow's cries as she fought to bring that precious life into the world.

Simon, James, Emma, Helena, Graham and Adelaide stood at the sideboard. The women were preparing tea for the group as a whole and everyone was smiling. Of course, two of them, as well as Meg, had gone through this ordeal that Charlotte now faced, and had come out healthy and with happy babies in their arms. Hugh and Robert stood to one side, both looking entirely uncomfortable.

And in the middle was Ewan, pacing the length of the room,

his hands shaking and his brow sweaty. Baldwin walked with him, saying soft words of comfort. Immediately, Isabel released Matthew and gave him a gentle push.

"Go," she said softly. "He needs no one in this room more than you."

He gave her a glance of thanks and then headed straight for his cousin. Ewan embraced him and she watched the two men interact, silent but as connected as the closest of brothers. Ewan didn't even pull out his little notebook. He and Matthew just held gazes and she could see they understood each other perfectly.

Tears filled her eyes as she moved to the place along the wall to wait with the others. After a moment, Helena slipped up beside her. Isabel stiffened, for the Duchess of Sheffield had been the only one to confront her directly, and Isabel wasn't certain what the woman would say now.

"Good afternoon, Isabel," Helena said, smiling at her with a true friendliness.

Isabel inclined her head. "Helena."

To her surprise, Helena slipped an arm through hers, and together they watched Baldwin, Ewan and Matthew for a moment. Ewan already seemed more relaxed with his friends at his side. His pacing was less manic, less fearful, though he continued to look toward the door every time even a peep came from Charlotte.

"They have been best friends since they were boys," Helena mused. "When I see them together, I am never unmoved by their connection."

Isabel nodded as she watched Matthew's face. He was Ewan's strength in that moment. The rock that allowed Ewan to buckle in his fear if he needed to do so.

"It is powerful," she whispered. "And rare."

"It *is* rare." Helena turned toward her. "And I would never do anything to interfere in it. I know I approached you before your marriage and spoke to you…rather harshly."

Isabel shook her head. "You were direct. I cannot fault you for that, nor for your protectiveness of Matthew."

Helena's expression softened and she gently squeezed Isabel's arm. "A protectiveness I now realize you share, I think. After all, you stood up for him in front of all his friends and family against your own uncle on your wedding day."

Isabel blushed. "He never should have been put in a position where he'd have to be defended from my uncle."

Helena tilted her head. "But this is the position he is in, and you. I just wanted to say that I saw how fervently you defended him. It meant a great deal to me, to all of us, that you would do so. I hope that you and I can be friends. Truly friends, since I know we will see each other often thanks to the bond our husbands share. And I know that if Charlotte weren't cursing the heavens just down the hall, she would say the same thing."

Isabel smiled and covered Helena's hand with her own. Relief flowed through her and a comfort at the idea that this woman, all these women, could accept and care for her.

"Yes," she said softly. "Of course I would be very happy to be your friend."

Suddenly there was another cry that cut through the air, but it wasn't Charlotte's. This time it was the keening wail of a baby. Isabel jolted, and both she and Helena turned their attention to the men. Ewan buckled at the sound of the baby. Matthew and Baldwin each caught his arms to keep him from collapse. Then the three moved in together, in a circle of brotherly love and relief.

When Ewan pulled away, it was clear from the tears streaming down his face that the voice of his healthy child had changed all his fear to joy.

Within a moment, Meg stepped into the room. She was beaming as she wiped her hands dry on a towel. "A boy," she declared to the cheers of the group. She moved to Ewan and touched his cheek. "A strong, *wailing* boy who is making himself very known at this moment. Mama and baby are right as rain."

Matthew shoved Ewan toward the door. "Go!" he declared. "Go see your little family."

Ewan did not have to be told twice. He rushed out as Meg crossed the room and fell into Simon's arms. Helena pulled away to go to Baldwin, and for a moment Isabel was alone. She watched from a distance as this group of friends, this club of dukes, this band of brothers, celebrating the addition of a new family member to their tight fold. She reveled in their tears and their smiles. In their celebration.

And she bathed in the warm realization that she would be some small part of this circle of love. That her children would grow up in it. That it would always be there to be depended upon and nourished. Perhaps she'd never be as accepted as the others, but Helena had made an overture, and that gave her hope that she wouldn't forever be an outsider.

Joy swelled in Matthew, but it was incomplete as he turned away from Baldwin and Helena. Along the wall, he found Isabel, standing away from the others, watching him. Just watching him.

In that moment, he wanted to share this happiness and relief with her more than any other person in that room. He came toward her, closing the distance in three long strides. She straightened at his approach, her expression both wary and open. There was nothing to say. He simply wrapped his arms around her and drew her hard against his chest as tears began to stream down his cheeks.

She pulled back a fraction and wiped at them. She was smiling, understanding that these were tears of happiness.

"I watched my cousin grow up so uncertain of his value," Matthew choked out. "Not even my father and mother's love, my love and acceptance, could make him forget the cruelty he suffered because of his lack of ability to speak."

She nodded slowly. "It must have been so hard for him."

"It was." Matthew shook his head. "Tonight, when his son

cried out and it was clear the boy will not suffer the same affliction, I saw all my cousin…my *brother's* fears fade away. I saw hope in him that I've never seen before."

"Not that the baby would have been any less loved were he unable to speak."

"Of course not. We could say that until we were blue in the face, though. None of us has walked Ewan's path or felt his terror of his child suffering as he did."

"But now that child will not," she said, touching his cheek once more. "The fact that you are so happy for him speaks volumes about you, Matthew. Your character and your capacity for love."

He stiffened at her use of that word. *Love.* It was something he'd cut away for so long. Something he'd told himself he could not and would not feel ever again after the loss that had dragged him to the depths of despair.

But today he felt it, powerful and beautiful and changing in the very best of ways. He felt it and sank into it as the men and women in the room around them shared in the joy of this happiest of days.

Looking at the woman beside him, he could not think of anyone else he'd rather share this day with. So he bent his head and kissed her. Not with passion, but something deeper. With the relief and joy that could flow so easily between them. He didn't care who saw that connection. He didn't care about how vulnerable it made him.

She pulled away at last and smiled, her cheeks bright with color. "I'm so happy for your family, Matthew."

"Our family," he corrected. "They're *our* family."

Her eyes went a little wider. And why not? Their marriage had been forced, their connection made tenuous by lies and misunderstanding. He'd offered her no glimpse at the future they would share, in part because he was having a hard time defining it for himself.

But in this moment, he knew that he would try. Try to make it happy. Try to make her happy. For the rest of their lives.

Because she deserved it. And after all he'd lost, so did he.

The birth of his cousin's child had signaled a new day for him. He intended to make the rest of their days even better.

CHAPTER TWENTY

Isabel sat on the edge of a chair in her uncle's parlor, staring nervously at the door he would soon enter through. After all the joy of the previous day, when Charlotte and Ewan's baby had joined the world to such happy fanfare, she had returned to the house to find a message from Uncle Fenton.

He had not contacted her since the ugliness they had exchanged at her wedding. She'd considered his silence a good sign. Perhaps he was cooling off, coming back to the rational man that she had to believe still lived inside of him.

The hope for that made her hide the message from Matthew and come here, uncertain of what she'd find. If her husband had insisted on coming with her, she would guess it would not have been good. She had to be an example for them both, opening doors between them behind the scenes, or at least steering each man away from anger and revenge.

It was her duty as someone who loved them both.

The door to the parlor opened and she rose as her uncle entered. She jerked her hand to her mouth. He was completely undone. In the ten days since she'd seen him, he had lost nearly a stone. His clothing hung off his already slender shoulders and there were deep circles beneath his eyes. He was sloppy and untucked, and he swayed slightly as he entered the chamber and speared her with a glance.

"Hello, Isabel," he slurred.

She flinched. "Uncle," she said softly. "You are drunk."

"Perhaps." He shrugged. "Doesn't really matter, does it? Drunk or sober, life is the same."

She frowned and came forward to take his arm. He allowed it and took the seat she guided him to. She smoothed a lock of hair away from his forehead and shook her head. "You must see you are out of control. You must see that you need some kind of…help."

For a moment he met her eyes. There was desperation there. Longing, like he might agree that he'd gone too far. But then he blinked and the anger he used as a shield against his pain returned.

"I do want your help. No one is talking anymore."

She sighed as she took a place on the settee. "Talking about what?"

He waved his hand at her wildly. "You. And him. At first it was all I'd hoped for. A scandal to bring him down a peg. But then you married and the talk faded."

"Yes, didn't the Countess of Longview leave her husband in some kind of public row in Hyde Park? I assume they are all atwitter about that."

He scowled. "It's as if what he did doesn't matter."

"Please listen to me," she said, scooting to the front of the settee and reaching out to take his hands. He flinched, but didn't pull away. She tilted her head to find his gaze and held it there. "Matthew didn't do anything."

"No," he said.

"He didn't," she repeated softly. "I have heard what happened that night and I believe his story."

"No!" he repeated, jumping to his feet. "But you are the only one who can reveal the truth now."

She bent her head. His drive, it had crossed into the realm of madness, and though she felt for him, pitied him, she was also tired of this argument and the accusations that went along with it.

"I'm telling you the truth." She got up. "You just don't want to listen."

"You are close to him now. It is repugnant, but we can use it." His eyes lit up.

Isabel stared. "Use it to what, exactly?"

"Spy on him. Force him to reveal his secrets."

She turned away, pacing to the window, where she gripped her fists at her sides and tried to regain a fraction of control over herself. Emotions bubbled up in her: pain and empathy, anger and defensiveness, and loss. So much loss, because it felt like she would never have her uncle back again. This man left in the wake of his grief was…not him.

She slowly faced him. "I want you to hear me, Uncle Fenton. Truly hear me. I understand your drive to avenge your daughter. I understand you believe, in your deepest heart, in the very corners of your soul, that Matthew is at fault for her loss. But that does not mean it's accurate. And I will not now, nor will I ever be party to causing him harm. Do I make myself clear?"

He stared at her, unspeaking, for what felt like an eternity. His gaze went blank at last and he got up. "Then you are of no use. I must only help myself. And I do not think we shall see each other again."

She caught her breath as renewed pain ripped through her. She had loved her uncle all her life. Nothing he had done or said had erased the kindnesses he had once shown her, or eliminated the many things they had in common. But he looked at her now like she was a stranger. And in turn, he was a stranger to her, too.

"If you cannot see reason, then perhaps that is best," she whispered. "I'll leave you now. Goodbye."

He hesitated, his frown deepening. Then he nodded. "Goodbye, Isabel. Goodbye."

She threw her shoulders back, trying to keep her dignity as she walked from the room. But when she had climbed back into her carriage, when she had started on her way back home, she couldn't help but slide down in the seat and cry.

Matthew heard Isabel enter the foyer and looked up from his book in surprise. She had been going to call on Sarah and told him to expect her to be gone for the afternoon. But it had been less than an hour since her departure.

Not that he minded her return. He was beginning to miss her when she wasn't there.

He set his book aside and stepped into the hall. "You are early," he said. "Come have tea with me."

She glanced away from Portman and toward him, and his stomach dropped. She had been crying. It was clear on her face as she trudged toward him.

"I may need something stronger than tea," she said as she lifted to her tiptoes to kiss his cheek.

He wrinkled his brow and followed her into the parlor, shutting the door behind them so they could have privacy. She sank onto the settee with a long, ragged sigh and covered her eyes with her hand. A thousand questions raced through his mind. What had happened? Why had she come home? What could he do to ease the pain that was so obvious in every fiber of her being?

He wanted to do so desperately.

So he started with a drink and poured her a sherry from the sideboard. When he handed it over to her, she laughed briefly. "I suppose now is as good a time as any to drink."

She took a sip and winced before she set the glass aside. He took a place next to her and took her hand, lifting it to his lips as he searched her unhappy face. "What happened?"

She flinched and her gaze darted away. He knew that look. He'd seen it so many times on her face. It was an expression of guilt, and his stomach clenched at the sight of it. He pushed the reaction aside.

"Did you quarrel with Sarah?" he asked, already knowing that wasn't the truth. Needing her to confess it regardless.

Needing to know that she would.

She didn't disappoint. "I didn't go to see Sarah," she admitted as she dropped her head. "I-I lied to you."

He gritted his teeth. "I thought we were past lies, Isabel. Are we not?"

"I know," she whispered, and her voice trembled with real pain that touched his heart even as he tried to close it off because she'd been untrue, yet again. "I was foolish. I thought I was protecting you."

He shook his head. "Protecting me? Where did you go?" She glanced at him and he sucked in a breath. "Your uncle. You went to see Winter."

She nodded slowly. "I received a summons from him yesterday, while we were away at Ewan and Charlotte's. In the excitement you didn't see it. I didn't want to upset you, and I didn't want you to interfere and have everything be worse. So I hid it and lied to you about where I was going."

He pushed to his feet and paced away. He was angry at the deception, of course, especially considering their history. But he also understood her motives in some way.

"You went alone to see him," he said at last. "I don't like that, Isabel. He is…"

"Unhinged," she finished for him, and it was on a sob.

He pivoted, and his heart softened. Her head was in her hands and she struggled with what was obviously great grief. Whatever he thought of Fenton Winter, whatever he had suffered at the blunt end of his accusations, he knew without a doubt that Isabel loved the man. She didn't agree with him or his terrible methods, but she did love him.

And seeing him unravel broke her heart. That mattered to Matthew. It mattered more than whatever anger he had that she would keep the truth from him.

He retook his seat and gathered her against him, holding her gently as he smoothed his hands along her trembling back and let her pour her pain into him. He took it all, holding her safe as she wept, and found himself comforted by the exchange. Her pain was easier to bear than his own in some ways. And taking it lessened its power.

When she had calmed, she looked up into his face. "I'm sorry," she whispered.

"Of course you are." He leaned forward to kiss her temple. "Now tell me what happened to so upset you."

She recited the details of the encounter slowly, and his heart sank with each one. What she was describing was truly a man on the edge. And while he had been threatening Matthew for years and Matthew was certain he would never actually follow through on any real plans, it was still disturbing to know that he was trying to wield Isabel as a weapon.

"I told him I would never involve myself in a plot to hurt you," she said at last. "And he told me we didn't need to see each other again."

He shook his head. "I'm sorry. I realize how much that must hurt you."

"It does," she admitted. "He was all the family I had left. There are a few cousins here and there, but I was never close to them. But I'm more afraid than anything."

"Why? Because he was trying, once again, to find a way to cause me grief?" he asked. "Darling, he's been doing that for so long, I hardly recall a time when he wasn't. I appreciate the concern, but there is no reason."

She grabbed for his arm and clung with both hands. "But Matthew—"

"Shhh," he soothed her, drawing her close again. "I promise you, there's nothing to fear. In truth, now that his last connection to me is severed, he might just settle back down. It could be for the best."

"I still think he's dangerous," she insisted. "I'm afraid for you."

He blinked as he looked down into her face. She was utterly serious in her concern for him. And the recognition of how deeply she cared, how driven she was to protect him, highlighted the closeness they had developed since the night at the Donville

Masquerade, a lifetime ago.

And even more surprising was how he felt the same for her. A drive to comfort her. Help her. Soothe her.

He slid his fingers along the curve of her jawline and dropped his lips to hers.

For a moment, the kiss was gentle. Sweet. But it swiftly deepened and moved toward the powerful physical connection they shared. He knew one way to make her forget everything but pleasure. And if the way she lifted against him was any indication, it was a way she wanted to explore, as well.

He dropped to his knees before her, cupping her cheeks as he continued kissing her. He could feel her smiling against his lips, trembling as her hands fisted against his arms. There was surrender in her taste and her soft sighs as he broke his mouth away and dragged it down her throat.

"Lay back," he ordered as he nudged his way between her legs with his shoulders and then began to slide her skirt up.

She looked like she might argue for one brief moment, but then she sighed, closed her eyes and rested her head back. She was trusting him completely with her body and her pleasure. He wanted to reward that trust. He wanted to grant her pleasure and take his own from watching her.

The skirt bunched at her knees and he leaned down to kiss each one in turn. She gasped and her eyes came open. She watched him kiss higher, his tongue tracing the inner line of her thigh as he parted her legs even farther.

When he pushed her skirt up over her stomach, he smiled and glanced up at her. "No drawers?"

She bit her lip and shrugged. "You said you wanted a little swan here and there."

"Here," he said, pressing his hand between her legs and smiling as she gasped in pleasure. She was already wet, and he parted her folds and spread the damp evidence of her desire across the hot opening of her sex. "And there."

She murmured some kind of incoherent reply, which he ignored as he adjusted himself into place and then dropped his mouth to her. She opened wider with a cry, her hands coming to grip his hair as he traced her sex, reveling in her sweet, clean flavor. In the way she lifted to meet every stroke as he tasted each inch of her body.

"Please," she murmured, her head thrashing on the settee as she lifted her hips to meet the strokes of his tongue. "Please, please."

He continued to toy with her, stoking the ever-burning fire of her desire. He was of two minds. If he focused on the slick bud of her clitoris, he could have her screaming out his name and bucking against his tongue in moments.

Or he could draw this out. Draw her out. Give her even greater anticipation before she finally exploded around him.

The second seemed the best option. He glided his tongue along her length, specifically avoiding the place where she needed him most. She rocked helplessly and glared down at him. He smiled against her skin and responded by pressing two fingers into her sheath.

She gripped him immediately, her heat drawing him as far as he could go. He curled his fingers, watching as she mewled and contorted against the pleasure. He went on like that, curling and licking, sucking and teasing, until her breath was short and her fists pounded against the settee cushions in a silent plea for release.

Gone from her beautiful face was any regret or pain. Forgotten was trouble and anxiety. For both of them. Giving her this moment of pleasure was certainly a great one for him. One he appreciated almost as much as the moments when her shaking body milked him to completion.

He nipped her clitoris gently and she bucked as her eyes went wide. She was nodding now, probably not even recognizing she was doing it. Encouraging him to give her what she needed. To free her from pleasurable torment at last.

So he did. He sucked her clitoris, rolling his tongue around and around the slick bud. She ground against him, her back arching nearly off the settee until finally her hips began to buck out of control. She thrashed, the rippling waves of her orgasm sucking his fingers even deeper as he drew the pleasure out until she flopped, spent and weak, on the settee cushions. Satisfied at last.

He leaned her body up, pulling her to him as he kissed her, let her taste the flavor of her pleasure. She wrapped her arms around his neck, probing his lips with her tongue with a lazy sensuality that came purely from her very good instincts.

She opened her eyes and held his stare. They were close now. Too close, he would have once said. Today, it felt exactly close enough.

"Take me upstairs," she whispered. "And let's do that again."

He grinned before he pressed his mouth hard to hers, tugged her into his arms, and did just that.

CHAPTER TWENTY-ONE

Matthew's neck had a crick. He grinned as he worked the pinched muscle with his hand and remembered exactly how he'd gotten it—hours with his wife, tangled with her in his bed as she arched beneath him in wild abandon. He'd left her there, soundly sleeping, her naked body spread across his sheets and ready for him when he finished with a few items on his to do list.

Something he raced to do now. Then he'd have to decide how he'd wake her. Tongue? Hands? Cock? So many possibilities.

In the distance, he heard a faint sound. A thud, and he frowned as he looked at the clock above his mantel. It was nearly three. Late for a servant to be up and about, though he wouldn't put it past Portman to already be seeing to the daily routine. The man never stopped.

It was silent now, though. Matthew bent his head back to his work. He'd ask the butler about it tomorrow. Perhaps Isabel could be part of the discussion. She would likely be able to charm him into taking a new schedule.

How could anyone deny her?

He dipped his quill into the pot of ink and scratched a few words along the vellum before him. He had nearly lost himself in the act when the door to his study clicked shut. He lifted his gaze and found himself looking down the barrel of a gun. A gun being held by Fenton Winter.

He jolted back against his chair, pushing away from the

weapon as far as he could go as he forced himself to look up at his attacker. Winter's hair was wild, his eyes were glassy, his hands shaking as he leveled the pistol at Matthew's head. He looked unwell and unbalanced, and none of that made this situation any less fraught with peril.

"W-Winter," Matthew stammered in shock. "What are you doing? How did you get in here?"

"I've watched you for so long," Winter said, his voice shaking like his hands. "I know there's a side door your butler sometimes accidentally leaves unlocked after deliveries. I've even used it once or twice before. Stepped into your house and stood in your pantry, then let myself out again. Just to know I could when I needed to." He motioned the weapon in Matthew's face. "Get up."

Matthew slowly lifted his hands and pushed his chair back from his desk. As he came around the furniture and stood face-to-face with Winter, he shook his head. He had spent so much time trying to convince Isabel that there was nothing to fear from her uncle, that his past actions would dictate all his future ones. It seemed he had been very wrong.

"I should have listened to her," he said softly.

Winter's eyes lit up. "Her. Angelica?"

"No, your niece," Matthew whispered. "Isabel."

Winter's gaze dropped a fraction, filled with guilt. "She will understand someday. I hope she'll understand."

"No."

Both men glanced toward the door, and Matthew's heart dropped. Isabel was standing there, wrapped in his robe, her hair down around her shoulders. Beautiful and his, but perhaps only for a few more moments. She was staring at her uncle, pleading in her eyes. Terror.

"Go upstairs, Isabel," Matthew said. "Please."

She shook her head. "I shall not," she said with firm determination.

"Do as he says," Winter barked.

She flinched at the angry tone, but didn't obey either of

them. Instead, she stepped into the room and toward them. Step by step, Matthew tracked her, tensing with every step until she wedged herself in front of him, her uncle's pistol now pressed into her chest instead of Matthew's.

"What are you doing?" Winter hissed. "Get out of the way."

"Isabel." Matthew grabbed her arm and tried to shove her aside, but she set her feet wide and tensed her body against him.

"Stop it, both of you," she said.

She lifted her chin and looked evenly at Winter. His hand shook even more, and Matthew tensed. If that gun fired, Isabel *would* die. There was no doubt. But she didn't stop. She didn't step away. And she didn't seem to care because she was determined to protect him.

And he realized, in that awful moment, that he loved her beyond measure. And he might lose her.

"What are you doing, uncle?" Isabel asked, and was proud that her voice sounded remarkably calm, considering what was happening.

"You wouldn't help me," Fenton said, his voice pleading as if he could make his case with her. "I can't wait anymore, I can't watch anymore, while he gets to go on and my Angelica is in a cold, dark grave all...all alone."

When his breath caught, she felt Matthew shift behind her. The pain both of them felt in that moment was palpable. Mirror images, though it had torn them apart. She wondered briefly it they could have helped each other, once upon a time. If her uncle hadn't resorted to anger, would they have been able to hold each other in their grief until they survived it?

Sadly, they would never know. Because here they were. And her uncle was determined to destroy Matthew.

"You will have to shoot me in order to take him," she said, the words like sandpaper in her throat. She meant them despite the terror they engendered deep within her, in some primal place that screamed at her to live no matter what.

The part that loved Matthew was stronger.

"Isabel!" Matthew hissed, his tone sharp and desperate behind her.

She ignored him and remained focused on Uncle Fenton. "Is that what you're willing to do?"

He stared at her. His eyes were glassy, but somewhere deep inside of him she still saw the flicker of his true self. The man he'd been before his child had been torn from him. The man who would never hurt her.

She had to believe *that* man would win over the one overcome by irrational hate.

"Please don't make me," he said, his hands trembling even more. She held her breath, for she knew that gun could fire at any moment.

"No one will make you become a murderer," she said. "You will have done that yourself. You will be a murderer. And *he* still won't be."

"He will. He is."

She shook her head. "He isn't. I loved Angelica, but I see her with a more realistic view, perhaps more than either of you. She was wonderful, and she could be petulant and spoiled and irrational. You remember when I won that scavenger hunt when we were twelve?"

Her uncle blinked, like he hadn't thought of Angelica as anything but a corpse for so long that a memory of her as a child seemed foreign. "She—she was angry. She threw your prize into the river."

She nodded. "She would have her way, no matter how ridiculous it was."

"She was a girl then," Fenton snapped, his angry gaze focusing on her. "It was different when she was older."

"Was it?" she asked, trying hard to hold her ground. Happy that Matthew was standing behind her, rigid with rage and terror, but allowing her this opportunity to end this night with no bloodshed. Like he...trusted her. "Is it truly so hard to believe that she would have a fit of pique over not getting her way? That she would take what she wanted regardless and do it without a thought to the consequences?"

Her uncle wavered a little, but she gasped at the sight of it. Her words were sinking in.

"I don't know," he whispered.

"You want to blame someone else because the pain is so deep, so powerful. So unyielding that the rage is all you have to keep it at bay. But if you kill Matthew, it will not change a damn thing about what you've lost. It will only turn you into a monster that your daughter would have turned away from in horror. Is that what you want? What you truly want? To kill this man Angelica loved? Who...I love."

Matthew tensed at her back, but she ignored him. If she was going to die protecting him, she needed him to know what she felt. If she lived, they could deal with the result later.

"Isabel," her uncle whispered, his tone heavy and mournful.

She continued, "Are you truly planning to destroy the last good thing in your daughter's life just to make yourself feel momentarily better?"

He stared at her, his eyes now full of a desperate plea for help. She saw it there, and she said, "Please, Uncle Fenton, put the gun down. Don't hurt me. Don't hurt him. It's all I ask of you."

His hand shook, harder than ever, and then he lowered the pistol and sank to his knees. Loud sobs racked him and she dropped down beside him, hugging him as she pushed the gun out of reach and let him cry. She looked up at Matthew, his eyes soft with pity and dark with fear and relief. He touched her shoulder, his fingers pressing into her before he strode to the door and rang the bell for Portman to come.

Matthew stood at the dim light of dawn that sparkled through the windows into his study. He had never been so happy to see another morning, to face another day and know that Isabel was still alive in it.

As if he had conjured her, she entered the room and came to a stop. He stared at her, with the shadows beneath her dark eyes, with the evidence of her tears still lined on her face, with her lower lip trembling. And then she made a soft sound and crossed the room to him. She fell into his arms, her entire body shaking as he held her. And he shuddered too as the gravity of what they'd just endured hit him squarely in the chest.

He had lost one woman he loved. To lose another would have killed him. He knew that. He felt it to the very bones in his body, and he crushed her closer out of pure protective instinct.

They stood there a moment and then he pulled away. "You are exhausted. Come sit by the fire."

She followed silently and settled onto the settee, resting her head on his shoulder as he smoothed his hands along her side. She let out a long, shuddering sigh. "You were kind not to report my uncle to the authorities," she said. "Kinder than perhaps he deserves."

He pressed his lips together hard. "I did it for you," he said. "And for her."

"Angelica," she whispered.

He nodded and pressed a kiss to her temple. "Where will they take him?"

She sat up and turned toward him. "They are distant cousins, but they were eager to help him. He'll go to the country for a while. It will be good for him to be away from his shrines. Perhaps he'll be able to sit through his grief at last and come out the other side to the man I once knew."

"I will ask for reports regularly," Matthew said, setting his jaw. "To be certain he never threatens you again."

She touched his face. "He was threatening you, Matthew. Not me."

"Hard to recall when the barrel of the gun was pressed into

your chest," he said, his tone sharper than he'd meant it to be. It was hard to meter it when the terror flared up again. "I should have listened to you when you warned me of his intentions. When I think of what could have happened. How I could have lost you…"

He trailed off, for he wasn't ready to voice those words out loud yet. They had too much power in his head.

"It must have brought back terrible memories," she said gently. "Of losing her."

He shook his head. "It wasn't memories that troubled me, Isabel. It was thinking about my future without you that drove me mad. It had nothing to do with Angelica."

Her lips parted and she stared at him, her face bright with disbelief. He hated to see it there, but why wouldn't it be? He hadn't let her in over the weeks they'd been thrown together. He hadn't trusted her or allowed the growing connection he felt toward her to flourish.

The love that he had realized almost too late.

He took her hand, smoothing his thumb over it as he tried to find the words to explain. He had to say those first, before he spent the rest of his life performing actions to prove himself to her. "You said something to me on our wedding night. Something that has weighed on my mind ever since."

She tilted her head. "What did I say?"

"You asked me what the chances were that we would find each other at the Donville Masquerade."

She shrugged. "It was an offhand comment, though."

"What *were* the odds, Isabel?"

She jolted at his insistence and shook her head. "One in a hundred, perhaps?"

"Perhaps one in a thousand," he offered. "There were dozens of steps that had to be taken by each of us so that we would both be taken to that place that night. The path was almost impossible."

"I don't understand, so it was chance, what about it?"

"It wasn't chance," he whispered.

She drew back, and her utter confusion was adorable and heartbreaking all at once. "What else would it have been, Matthew? You said you believed I didn't plan the encounter, I know you didn't. So how could it be anything but chance?"

"Angelica," he said.

She tensed and tugged at her hand, but he held fast. She couldn't run now, he couldn't let her. Not until she understood that he wasn't comparing her to the woman he'd lost.

"She loved me," he said. "And she loved you. Is it so hard to believe that she might look at us from the beyond and want us to find each other?"

Her bottom lip had begun to tremble again. "Why? For what purpose?"

"Because she knew we could love each other," he suggested.

Her eyes went wide. There it was, sinking in, a better understanding of what he was implying. Of what he wanted and needed from her. But she still didn't quite have faith. Doubt still ruled.

"Don't," she whispered.

He touched her chin. "Look at me."

She faced him, her lips pressed together, her hands clenched against his.

"I love you, Isabel."

Matthew's words were like the shot to her heart her uncle hadn't taken, and she recoiled from their power. But he wouldn't let her run. He held her gently, watching her, waiting for her to steady herself.

Waiting for her to believe what was entirely impossible. A dream that she had accepted would never be reality.

But he offered it to her now. Why? She didn't know, but she feared it was not because those feelings were true.

"You are overwrought," she said past a thick tongue. "You are grateful you didn't die and feel obligated because I stepped between you and my uncle."

He smiled. "I am not overwrought."

"You are—"

"Very well, if you believe that then I shall simply take you upstairs and make love to you in my heightened emotional state, and tomorrow I will start this conversation over. If it doesn't work then, I will try the next morning and the next and the next." He cupped her cheeks. "Until you *believe me*."

Her heart swelled as he brushed his nose against hers, gentle. Intimate. Sweet and so loving. Almost enough that she could have faith in what he said.

"I don't understand," she said at last. "How could you love me?"

He drew back a fraction. "The better question is, how could I not? You are…everything, Isabel. Intelligent and kind, strong beyond measure, even to a fault, as you proved today. You are beautiful and alluring. You have awakened all the best parts of me, even the ones I thought no longer existed. You make me want to *live*. To wake up every day and see you across my breakfast table, to dance with you at balls, to bring you home…or even sometimes to the Donville Masquerade if you'd like to be very naughty, and make love to you."

She blushed hot even as his words seared into her soul. Could she believe them? Believe him?

He shook his head. "I realize I have given you no reason to return my feelings. I recognize your declaring yourself earlier was a ploy to stop your uncle."

She couldn't hold back the bark of laughter at the very idea. "A ploy? No, not at all. From the first moment a stranger stepped between me and a man bent on harm and destruction, I have been falling in love with him. With you." She stared at him. What he was suggesting was the greatest risk, the greatest leap she would ever take. But with the biggest payoff of all. "I-I love you," she said.

"You do?" he repeated, and sounded just as confused as she had felt just a few moments before.

"Yes!" she burst out, and began to laugh. Because there was so much joy to be had and happiness, so much light in the future they'd share. "Must I prove it?"

His eyes lit up and he dragged her closer. Into his lap and his arms and fully into his life. He smiled. "I think so."

She wrapped her arms around his neck and pressed her forehead to his as all the joy in the world filled her. "With pleasure," she murmured before she claimed his lips.

EPILOGUE

Three month later

Isabel sat in Ewan and Charlotte's parlor. She was meant to be playing whist with the other duchesses, women she had come to see as friends, sisters. Instead, she was staring across the room at her husband.

Matthew perched Ewan and Charlotte's baby, Jonathon, in his arms. He looked utterly terrified, like at any moment the baby would burst into flames or hurtle from his arms. She laughed at the expression and the care and love that was behind it.

She smiled at her friends as she laid down her last card and then got up to cross the room to her husband. He looked relieved as he handed the baby off to Baldwin and reached out to take her arm.

"Need a little air?" she asked, guiding him toward the terrace and away from all the ears in the parlor.

He nodded and took a long sigh. "I have no idea what to do with a baby, I swear. Am I supposed to be comfortable? I do not feel comfortable."

She couldn't help but laugh at his nervous ramblings. Then she touched his face. The past month had been utterly blissful. There was no mistaking his love for her, or his passion. There was no hiding her own. And with that acceptance, their future looked so very bright.

"You'll have several months to practice with all the children of our friends, I suppose," she said, raising her eyebrows at him. "And I think most papas are more comfortable with their own, at any rate."

He blinked, staring at her blankly as he tried to digest what she meant. Then his mouth dropped open. "Are you telling me you are pregnant?"

She nodded, and before she could ask if he was happy, he caught her in his arms and spun her around the terrace with a whoop of pleasure. She laughed as she dropped her mouth to his. What had started with a secret, a mask, a lie…was now more than she ever would have dared hope for.

And she couldn't wait for the next chapter of her life with him.

Enjoy an exciting excerpt from

The Duke who Lied

out August 2018

Hugh swung down from his horse, jerking out a nod at the servant who rushed down to take the animal. With a long sigh, he looked up at the fine estate before him. His London estate, though it had never fully felt like his. None of the estates felt like they were, no matter how long he had been duke. It still felt like he was living a stolen life. A fraud who would be discovered at any moment when his own father returned from the dead.

How disappointed he would be in his son. Hugh knew that more than he knew anything in the world.

The door to the house opened and his longtime butler, Murphy, stepped out. Hugh forced himself out of the melancholy that had tracked his every move for over a year and climbed the steps two at a time to reach his servant.

"Welcome home, Your Grace," Murphy intoned as he took Hugh's hat and gloves. "I hope your trip to Brighthollow was most excellent."

Hugh barely contained his flinch at the benign words. He'd been at his country estate in Brighthollow for the past fortnight, tending to a bit of business and checking in on Lizzie. He'd begged her to come to London with him. She had refused.

After her ordeal the previous spring, she had not been the same. It felt like she was folding up into herself and there seemed to be nothing at all he could do about it.

"Uneventful," he choked out, since Murphy was awaiting the barest politeness of a response. "Is there anything to report here?"

He began to walk toward his study, the butler keeping up with him at his heels. "You've several invitations from the members of your club, Your Grace."

Hugh nodded. Of course he would. Since he was a boy he'd been the best of friends with a small group of men all destined to be dukes. The 1797 Club, they called themselves. He adored them all, but he could see the concern on their collective faces when he called on them. They knew something was wrong, he just hadn't the heart yet to tell any of them the truth.

How could he? How could he reveal his sister's deepest shame, how could he tell these men of honor that he had done nothing to the man who had hurt her? They'd say they understood, of course. They would, on some level. And yet he would feel his failure all the more if he dared speak it out loud.

So he kept it to himself and ignored their questions when they asked why he brooded, why he'd let his hair grow out and only shaved when Society required it. Why he hid in his castle in Brighthollow or his chambers here in London like a wounded beast.

"I shall look at them. I assume you left them on my desk?" he asked as they entered the study together.

"Of course." Murphy indicated the small silver tray on the corner of Hugh's desk, the one now brimming with correspondence in a variety of hands he knew so well.

He ignored them and came around to his seat. As he took it, he glanced up at Murphy. "If there isn't anything else…"

Murphy cleared his throat. "Only two pressing matters, Your Grace."

Hugh arched a brow. "And what is that."

"You told me to treat any messages from Mr. Kendall as urgent. One arrived for you yesterday."

Hugh pushed back from his desk, his chair making a screech on the wooden floor that caused his butler to turn his face in displeasure. "Kendall?" he repeated. "Where is it?"

He grabbed for the tray and began to slide his fingers through the letters there, shoving aside the ones from his friends in the search.

"Here, Your Grace," Murphy said, his tone suddenly

hushed, concerned as he dug into his inside pocket and drew out a folded piece of vellum, sealed with red wax. "I-I held it aside for you."

Hugh snatched it and turned it over. His name was spelled incorrectly. But he hadn't hired the man for his letter writing skills. "That will be all," he said, his voice shaking as he turned it back and grabbed for his letter opener to break the seal.

"Your Grace, there is one other thing-"

"No!" Hugh waved him off impatiently. "It can wait. Thank you, Murphy."

The butler nodded and saw himself out, shutting the door firmly behind him. Once he had, Hugh rushed to the fire and took a seat there. It was a short message, thank God, for Kendall truly was a terrible writer. His handwriting was barely legible and his poor spelling made Hugh have to re-read each sentence to pick out its meaning.

But there it was, in the end, in black and white. The nightmare Hugh had been waiting for the moment he hired Kendall over a year ago.

Other Books by Jess Michaels

THE 1797 CLUB

For information about the upcoming series, go to
www.1797club.com to join the club!

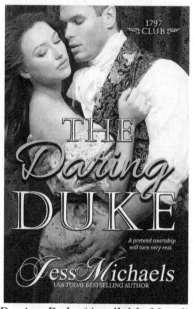

The Daring Duke (Available Now!)
Her Favorite Duke (Available Now!)
The Broken Duke (Available Now!)
The Silent Duke (Available Now!)
The Duke of Nothing (Available Now!)
The Undercover Duke (Available Now!)
The Duke Who Lied (Coming August 2018)
The Duke of Desire (Coming October 2018)
The Last Duke (Coming November 2018)

SEASONS

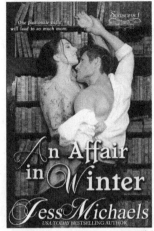

THE WICKED WOODLEYS

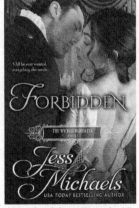

About the Author

USA Today Bestselling author Jess Michaels likes geeky stuff, Vanilla Coke Zero, anything coconut, cheese, fluffy cats, smooth cats, any cats, many dogs and people who care about the welfare of their fellow humans. She watches too much daytime court shows, but just enough Star Wars. She is lucky enough to be married to her favorite person in the world and live in a beautiful home on a golf course lake in Northern Arizona.

When she's not obsessively checking her steps on Fitbit or trying out new flavors of Greek yogurt, she writes historical romances with smoking hot alpha males and sassy ladies who do anything but wait to get what they want. She has written for numerous publishers and is now fully indie and loving every moment of it (well, almost every moment).

Jess loves to hear from fans! So please feel free to contact her in any of the following ways (or carrier pigeon):

www.AuthorJessMichaels.com

Email: Jess@AuthorJessMichaels.com
Twitter www.twitter.com/JessMichaelsbks
Facebook: www.facebook.com/JessMichaelsBks

Jess Michaels raffles a gift certificate EVERY month to members of her newsletter, so sign up on her website: http://www.authorjessmichaels.com/

Made in the USA
Monee, IL
02 October 2023

43857458R00132